Hawthorn and Mistletoe

C. Marie Bowen

Hawthorn and Mistletoe by C. Marie Bowen
Copyright © 2015 C. Marie Bowen
All rights reserved.

ISBN:1-945215-01-1
ISBN-13:978-1-945215-01-8

Edited by Liette Bougie
Cover Design by C. Marie Bowen
Published by Pixler Publications

Discover other titles by C. Marie Bowen at
www.cmariebowen.com

This is a work of fiction. Names, characters, places
and incidents are either products of the author's
imagination or are used fictitiously. Any
resemblance to actual events or persons, living or
dead, is entirely coincidental.

DEDICATION

This one is for Kyle.

CONTENTS

CHAPTER ONE

Well after sunset, Jurian Locke left the empty road to London and slipped into the dark forest. Near enough to hear movement along the road, yet distant enough to go unnoticed by any passerby, he lowered the bag from his shoulder and unbuckled the scabbard and sword from his back. After a long pull on his water skin, he wrapped his cloak around his shoulders and eased himself to the ground. His broad back rested against a sturdy tree while his mind sought ease in the moon's reflection in the Thames.

It was the end of the year 1328, and he received the chill, but dry December night as a Yule blessing from Odin. Perhaps the dry weather would hold for King Edward's Christmas Tournament and feast at Westminster two days hence. The retinues from several noble households, eager to demonstrate their strength before the young king's court, had passed by him earlier in the day.

Jurian tipped his head back, closed his eyes and listened to the river gurgle its way toward London. He planned to enter the lists as a man-at-arms and

1

perhaps win a purse at one or two of the competitions. Even though most mercenaries hoped to take service with a noble house during the tournament, Jurian had neither the expectation nor the desire to be bound in service. He'd already been bonded by love and magic to Agaria sim Biraci nearly 1400 years ago.

Although centuries had passed, the memory of that night refused to fade. Despite his father's wish for him to take the Druidess Nescato as his mate, his passion for Agaria could not be forsworn.

When Nescato had discovered Agaria in his arms, the Druidess had cursed them. Bitter with jealousy, she raised her bone staff, decorated with feathers and small skulls, pointed the stave at the couple, and evoked a curse that changed his life.

"For this deceit, I curse you to love only her for all eternity—in whatever form she is reborn. You will watch her die a thousand times, knowing your life goes on. Bound to her call, you will never rest in the slumber of death's arms. Your torment shall be everlasting."

Her head thrown back, Nescato had laughed as the wind whipped fallen leaves around her.

Jurian startled awake from the dream of Nescato's hate-filled eyes and gazed unseeing at the dark water until the sound of blade on blade and a warning shout drew his attention. Leaving his bag, he pulled his sword from its scabbard and came to his feet. The morning light filtered through the trees as he trampled over the forest brush and onto the road.

A small group of men, their coat of arms covered, set upon an old man and attacked his servants.

With a savage cry, Jurian moved forward and blocked the arc of the sword aimed to cleave the elderly man in half. Jurian's size alone daunted men, but his battle cry froze the assailants in their tracks.

The brigand blocked Jurian's swing and fell back a step. Piecemeal leather armor and hauberk proclaimed the attacker a mercenary man-at-arms, like himself.

Jurian swung again, and the sharp ring of metal filled the air. "Leave off, or I will see you dead." He pushed the man away and advanced, prepared to strike again.

The man blocked Jurian's next blow and staggered back. "Retreat," he called to the other assailants as he skirted around the carthorses. The group of thieves disappeared into the thick forest on the other side of the road.

A young retainer helped the elderly man to his feet. Of the age to be a squire, the lad dusted dirt from the old man's arm and wiped the filth from his hands onto his own chausses. He shoved fine brown hair from his face and tipped his head way back to look up at Jurian—mouth parted and eyes wide.

The master patted the youth's arm. "I'm well, Maury, thanks to this brave man." The white-haired man stood tall and straight as he nodded to Jurian, but spoke to his lad. "Where is Sir Reginald?"

"Here."

Jurian lowered his sword and followed the voice to the back of the wagon.

The injured knight had pulled himself to the wheel of the cart. Blood covered his face, and he held his arm awkwardly against his body.

"They came at me from behind and knocked me from Zeus." Reginald grimaced with pain. "I landed on my shoulder."

Jurian dropped his sword beside the knight and knelt to inspect the wound on his head. "They could have struck a killing blow from behind, had that been their intent. The cut to your scalp is wide but not deep."

"Your name, sir?" Reginald asked with a nod to Jurian's assessment.

"Jurian Locke."

"He saved me, Reggie," the older man affirmed. "One of the brigands had me down. This man came from behind the trees and halted the blow."

Jurian moved his inspection from Sir Reginald's head to his shoulder. "Your shoulder is disjointed from the fall."

"Aye."

"Did they take Zeus?" Maury asked.

"They may have tried," Reginald replied as he watched Jurian examine his shoulder.

Jurian's gaze rose to meet Reginald's. "This joint must be set in place."

Reginald nodded. "Can you do it?"

"I can, but you won't like it."

"Not much about this ambush I do like. Set it."

Jurian lifted Reginald's elbow and rotated his arm to align the joint. With a quick jerk, the bone slid back into the socket.

Reginald barked a cry of pain, then rested his bloody head against the wheel. "Thank ye, Jurian Locke."

Maury jumped from the cart with bandages as a rustling in the woods made Jurian reach for his blade.

From the forest, came a white destrier, blood dripping from its mouth. The horse stopped near Reginald, lowered his head and bared his teeth at Jurian.

Reginald lifted his good hand to the animal. "Peace, Zeus. He's a friend."

The old man took the bandages from Maury and tipped his head to Jurian. "Thank you for your aid, sir. I fear the brigands would have taken all and our lives." He held out his open hand. "My name is Sir Albert Clavel, an old knight who's lived past his usefulness. Reggie was once my squire." He pulled a linen from the bag, folded it, and pressed it firmly against Reginald's head wound. "You travel to London for the season's last tournament?"

"I do. I hope to win a purse or two in the competitions."

"We also travel to Edward's Tournament. Reggie planned to win the joust and be proclaimed Tournament Champion to seek a boon for me from the king." Albert wound the bandage around Reginald's head and tied it off. "Now I fear the lists will not see Sir Reginald's name."

"A stroke of luck for Piers Ramsey," Reginald muttered as Jurian helped him to his feet.

"Who is Ramsey?" Jurian asked.

"Son of Lord Milton Ramsey and suitor to Lady Elena Gregory, daughter of the Earl of Hawthorn." Albert tipped his head to Jurian. "Perchance, our attackers were friends of Ramsey." Albert rubbed his chin then lifted his brow at Reginald.

"If they were, they may be back. If so, we shall be easy meat for those vultures with my arm in a sling." Reginald stroked Zeus to calm the still agitated horse.

"I'll stay with you and see you safe to the tournament grounds." Jurian picked up his sword and motioned toward the woods on the far side of the road. "Let me first retrieve my things and we may be off."

Jurian's long stride took him back to his resting

place beside the Thames. He slid his sword, *Baraca*, into its scabbard and strapped the belt around his chest. He lifted his bag and returned to the knights.

Maury took Jurian's bag as he emerged from the trees and placed it in the cart.

Reginald walked the destrier to Jurian. "He won't be led, not Zeus. He must be ridden."

Jurian raised one eyebrow at Reginald. "Do you suggest I ride this savage mount?"

"You must. Maury is too small, and Albert drives the wagon." Reginald laughed and then grimaced in pain as he pulled Zeus's head down to rub between his ears. "I have not the strength to command him." He grinned at Jurian. "He needs a firm hand, but with my permission, he may allow you to mount."

Jurian eyed Zeus as he pulled at the reins in Reginald's hand and huffed at Jurian.

"Don't let him daunt you," Reginald joked. "He can smell fear."

"I'm not worried, but I don't want to hurt your mount."

"What do you mean?"

"If he bites me, I'll bloody his nose."

At that moment, Zeus bared his teeth and snapped at Jurian.

Reginald yanked down on the bit and glared into the horses eyes. "Stop this, Zeus."

"Give me the reins." Jurian leaped into the

saddle and gave a nod to Reginald.

The injured knight moved backward as Zeus rose on his hind legs in an attempt to unseat the heavy rider.

"He's not used to your size." Reginald grabbed the bit again and pulled Zeus's head down. "Settle, Zeus."

"I've got him." Jurian tightened the reins and turned the horses head sharp to the right.

Reginald grimaced as he made his way to the back of the cart. "Damned fine way to ride into London, in the back of this little tumbrel."

"Better led than dead," Sir Albert called back and shook the reins.

Albert gave Jurian several curious looks as they continued toward London. Finally, he waved Jurian over to the wagon. "Jurian Locke, I have a proposal for you."

Jurian studied the old warrior. "And that is?"

"Fight under my banner and add the joust to your efforts. You'll keep the purses from the events you win. If you are proclaimed the Tournament Champion and obtain the king's boon for me, then Zeus shall be yours.

Sir Reginald swung his head toward Sir Albert. "You'd forfeit Zeus?"

Jurian grinned. "Why would I want this stubborn horse? No." Jurian shook his head. "I'm better on the field than I am at the joust," Jurian warned.

"Besides, I'm not a knight. I doubt they'll allow my name on the lists. You'd do better to seek elsewhere for a knighted warrior to carry your banner."

"Perhaps," Albert muttered. "Then again, I'd wager you're better at both than most. I see how well you ride."

Jurian fell back as Sir Albert grumbled to Maury over the fates. Sir Albert's offer was not without merit. A horse, even one as bad tempered as Zeus, would carry him further in a day than he could manage on foot. He lowered his voice and addressed Sir Reginald, "What does Sir Albert want with the king's boon?"

"Ah," Sir Reginald sighed and shifted uncomfortably. "'Tis for a woman. What else?"

"Truly?" Jurian eyed the grizzled old knight at the front of the cart.

"Well," Sir Reginald whispered. "He fears to be alone in his dotage and desires an heir to warm his knee." They had ridden in silence for several paces before Reginald raised his head. "I plan to leave Sir Albert's service in the spring. I've lands of my own near Wales and a woman who I hope still waits." His attention shifted to Jurian. "Have you ever longed for the woman you love?"

The memory of Agaria's face bled across Jurian's vision. Her dark eyes reflected in an evening fire as she bit her lip and tipped her head toward the darkness beyond the flickering light.

Their desire for each other forbidden—their love undeniable.

"Aye," He whispered, and rubbed his face. "I've loved a woman."

Her touch, as soft as butterfly wings, her scent, a sweet musk.

He also remembered each time Agaria's life passed from this world and how many different loving eyes he'd laid to rest. Then he would face the countless years of waiting that followed. As he waited now.

It's been too long since her last call.

Perhaps Nescato's curse had become a curse of endless waiting. Or worse, to sense Agaria's need and have the summons cut short. Her death, somewhere to the east or west—beyond his reach—and then another lifetime of waiting would begin.

He examined the muscular animal between his legs.

Zeus would carry me swiftly to Agaria at her summons.

Jurian urged the mount forward to pace beside Sir Albert. "If they allow my name on the jousting list, I will fight for you. If I win the tournament, I shall gift the boon to you and take the purse and Zeus as my reward."

"We'll have to find armor that fits, and plead our case for your entry. God's teeth but you're a large man." Albert's grin split his face from ear to ear.

They rode for a time in silence and listened to Reginald's complaint about the bumpy road.

"Your boon," Jurian asked. "What is it you'll ask from King Edward?"

"I wish to marry young Elena Gregory. I would like an heir before I pass."

CHAPTER TWO

Elena Gregory sat straight-backed and still as Kelsey, her maid, brushed and plaited her long blonde hair into a thick braid down her back. Elena twined her fingers in her lap as Kelsey hummed a soft melody.

Elena couldn't help but worry about attending the festival games and the long walk across the field to the stands.

I worry about the smallest things.

It kept her from thinking about larger concerns that were out of her hands, like who her father would have her marry. A tolerant man by nature, her father, the Earl of Hawthorn had reached the end of his patience.

Kelsey completed Elena's appearance with a fine netted half-cap. She bound the netting at the base of Elena's hair and threaded satin ribbons through her thick braid to the bottom. On Elena's crown, she placed a golden fillet to keep the cap in place at the back of her head.

"There, my lady," Kelsey said. "I have finished."

Elena rose unsteadily to her feet and reached for

her crutch. A single piece of wood carved to fit beneath her arm and support her right leg. Her anklebone had never knit properly from her fall down the tower stairs as a child. It pained her to bear her full weight on that leg.

All in all, I think it pains father more.

Her dark-blue wool over gown had long trumpet sleeves embroidered with golden thread. The outer garment was corseted loosely over her light blue kirtle, a loose wool shift, cinched at the waist with matching embroidered ribbons. Elena nodded to her companion. "Thank you, Kelsey."

A short knock on the door silenced any further discussion between the young women. Elena's stepmother, Heloise, and father, Warner Gregory, the Earl of Hawthorn, entered her room.

"Ah good, you're ready." Her father's brow furrowed as his gaze fell to the crutch. "Must you bring that stick?"

"Only if I wish to walk," Elena replied and took an unsteady step forward. She sighed in exasperation at her father's frown. "It's only stiff from sitting. I'll move easier on the field."

"I hope so. Two offers for your hand and both barely acceptable. You must do better, Elena," her father scolded. "Be gay. Laugh. Lord knows a studious woman is difficult enough without—" He pointed to her leg.

"I shall do my best, father." Elena bowed her

head.

Heloise placed a comforting hand on her husband's arm. "Go down and ready the carriage, Warner. I'll help Elena down the stairs," Heloise said.

Her husband nodded and quit the room. His swift footsteps sounded on the stairs.

"I don't mean to annoy him." Elena looked at her stepmother.

"You don't, my dear. At least not directly. Your father is under some pressure from the Queen Mother and Mortimer to secure an heir to his title." Heloise hung her head. "If he's annoyed by anyone, I believe his displeasure should fall on me. I'm surprised he hasn't set me aside." She picked up more ribbons from the vanity and tied them around Elena's cane.

Elena grinned at the decorations on her walking stick and lifted her gaze to her step-mother. "He loves you, Heloise. He would never do that, and he's right, I've not done my best to secure a good husband." She took a faltering pace toward the door. "However, Father will get no heir from me with either Sir Albert Clavel or Piers Ramsey as my husband."

Heloise gripped Elena's arm and helped her down the stairs. "I understand Sir Clavel may be a bit aged to provide an heir, then again, consider Lord Umbridge. He's seventy if he's a day, with two babes at his wife's teats."

Elena shrugged and steadied her crutch when they reached the base of the stairs. "Perhaps." She shook her head at her stepmother's amused grin.

Heloise hid her dark hair beneath a silken wimple and veil, secured by a golden fillet. Her easy smile and blue eyes showed no concern that the Earl of Hawthorn would set her aside for another. Elena's father loved this woman and no wonder. Kindness flowed from Heloise to everyone around her.

Heloise smoothed her gown straight and spoke over her shoulder to Elena as she walked away. "Piers Ramsey could certainly get you with child. He's only slightly older than you, and you've known him all your life."

Elena and Kelsey exchanged a quick look.

Kelsey tipped her head and backed away. "My lady."

"Thank you, Kelsey." Elena followed Heloise out the door.

The Earl of Hawthorn maintained a small house in London but preferred to dwell at his larger estate in Essex. For King Edward's Christmas Tournament, he insisted Elena and Heloise accompany him to the festivities in London. His intentions were clear. Elena needed an acceptable suitor.

The rounded cloth covering on the carriage displayed the Hawthorn coat of arms on each side.

The attendant helped Heloise and Elena into the wagon, and then Warner climbed in and closed the low door. Before long, they passed through a city of tents that had sprung up around the Westminster Tournament field.

Elena searched the pennons for any she might recognize.

There are so many.

When the carriage approached the field, she spotted the Ramsey crest.

But Piers is no knight, nor is his father.

Before she could ask her father about the Ramsey tent, the carriage came to a halt.

A royal attendant opened the carriage door. "Good day, My Lord." The servant moved back as the Earl climbed from the conveyance and turned to help his wife.

"You have been assigned seats in the south pavilion, Lord Hawthorn."

Her father eyed the attendant as he helped Elena from the carriage. "The south, you say?"

"Yes, My Lord. Excellent seats with a view of the trebuchet and catapult competitions. I'm sure My Lord will be pleased."

A young page, perhaps eleven or twelve years old, approached the group. His outfit mirrored the coach attendant's royal livery. The youth made a formal bow to her father. "This way, My Lord." He turned, and with a skip in his step, led them across the grounds toward the south pavilion

Elena lagged behind her father and stepmother, walking carefully so she wouldn't trip and further embarrass herself and her family.

Her father waited for her and then took her arm. "Did you recognize any banners as we passed through the field of tents?"

"Only the Ramsey crest."

"I wasn't aware Ramsey had taken in the service of a knight," her father replied.

Heloise waited for them at the pavilion stair. "Perhaps, Ramsey retained one for the festival, Warner."

"Perhaps."

Their seats were in the third row, designated by a small pennon with the Hawthorn crest. Elena took her seat and slid her crutch beneath the wooden bench.

"This is the last day of the tournament, is it not?" Heloise asked her husband.

Warner nodded. "There have been several trials leading up to today's final events. Even the knights who have been eliminated remain for the melee tournament. The winning team will divide a cash prize and receive tournament points."

In front of the south pavilion stood a large trebuchet and catapult. Both war machines targeted a dirt field far to the east of the south stands. As each team came forward, they would adjust and load the weapons, then fire the stone mortars. An official wearing the king's livery marked their distance and made a note in his journal.

Beyond the machines, an earthen bank formed the edge of the melee grounds. At each end, a large hill of sod and rock held a different colored flag, one red and one blue.

Seated in the center pavilion, the royal family commanded a view of both venues. The north pavilion would observe only the melee tournament easily. Between the pavilions, peasants, merchants and craftsmen vied for a view along the fence line or sold their wares to the eager spectators.

The sudden whoosh and clank of the trebuchet caught their attention. The stone missile flew far into the field, landed, and rolled some distance.

Elena leaned toward Heloise as the official mark off the distance. "I had no idea they could throw that far."

"Come, my dear." Warner stood and took Heloise by the hand. "I would like to pay our respects to His Majesty and the Queen Mother before the melee begins."

Heloise rose and addressed Elena, "When we return, we'll bring a flagon of sweet wine."

Her father escorted Heloise along the bench row and down the steps. The couple disappeared into the sea of faces pressed between the nobles' seating areas.

The three pavilions were covered by bright-colored awnings, shading the sun from spectator's eyes. Banners hung around the fenced area, displaying familial coat of arms and festive seasonal pageantry.

The northern pavilion may have been the better seat, were Elena anxious to observe the melee. Although which seats were best would be hard to determine since the large gentleman in front of her stood and cheered each time the war machines fired. From where she sat, Elena could see nothing at all.

CHAPTER THREE

"This helm will not fit Jurian's head, Maury." Sir Albert tossed the metal helmet at the young squire. "Hurry and find another."

Maury ducked from the tent at a run.

Sir Reginald chuckled as he swirled the wine in his goblet. "Locke, you're too damned big."

In his padded jacket and leather breeches, Jurian rubbed his hand over his short hair. "I don't need a helm for the melee, Albert. A chain mail coif, a hauberk, and my own leather will suffice."

Maury dashed into the tent and skidded to a stop beside the table. "This is the largest helmet I could find." He dropped the heavy coat of mail on the table then handed Jurian the coif. "Will it fit?"

Jurian fitted the coif over his head and settled it on his brow and around his neck. "This will do, Maury. My thanks."

"And the coat?"

Jurian removed the coif and slid his arms into the hauberk. He lifted the ring mail and pushed his head inside.

Maury adjusted hauberk along Jurian's chest. "It

looks like a good fit."

"It's wide enough across the shoulders, and that's what matters." Jurian pulled the coif into place and reached for his leather gauntlets.

"Let me help you, sir." Maury laced the heavy leather gauntlets up Jurian's forearms and then picked up the red jerkin. "You've been assigned to defend the red pennon, sir."

Jurian bent and allowed Maury to place the sleeveless coat over the coif, settle the simple colored garment over his shoulders, and lace up the sides.

Reginald handed him his shield with the Clavel crest on the front. "Don't forget this."

The three knights emerged from Albert's tent and made their way to the entry gate.

Teams of blue and red knights formed lines, ready to enter the field.

The melee official walked between the rows of men, inspecting armor and weapons. "All weapons must be blunted or wrapped. No sharp edges permitted." He stopped at Jurian and pointed to the rack of blunted swords and clubs. "Choose one of these."

Jurian inspected the blunted game weapons and chose a sword similar in weight to *Baraca*. "This will suffice."

The official walked back to the front of the lines. "You will make your entrance in two rows. Your captains will lead you in." He nodded to the first man in each line who wore a bright yellow armband on their right arms. "You will bow before King Edward and then move to the flag that matches your jerkin. Your captain will only have a few moments to speak with you and form your team strategy. When the trumpet sounds, you shall advance on your opponents."

Jests and jibes flew back and forth between the lines while they waited. Unlike the fierce tournaments Jurian had participated in years before, Edward's tournament was played for sport—a game of tactics to please the crowd. Loss of life, at any of the events, would be frowned upon.

"Who's the big fellow at the end of your line, Chessam? A Viking giant?"

The Red Team's captain viewed the line and met Jurian's gaze. "A giant, verily. An adequate defense against your scrawny lads."

The Blue Team beat their blunted weapons against their shields and growled at the Red Team.

Reginald chuckled. "I wish I was well enough to participate. This looks to be great fun."

"Me too, lad," Albert said to Reginald. Albert clapped his hand against Jurian's shoulder. "We'll cheer you from the north fence line."

A trumpet on the other side of the barrier sounded, and the gate swung wide. The melee official led the procession of fighting men onto the field to the sound of the cheering crowd. They paraded in front of the north pavilion, then presented themselves to King Edward.

"Your Majesty." The official bent over his arm to the king. He straightened and threw his hands wide. "May I present the melee a pied, for your enjoyment." He lowered his head again, his face nearly touching his outstretched leg.

Jurian bowed with the other men then followed the Red Team toward the south side of the field.

Sir Chessam pointed to three men. "G'wean, Nash, and Fowler—you'll form our offensive. Kenyon, Dunham, Smyth and I will flank." He eyed Jurian. "My giant and Turney will guard our pennon. The rest of you spread out and cover the field. Let no one pass your position."

Jurian grinned at Sir Chessam. "Your giant's name is Jurian Locke."

Sir Turney laughed and beat his wrapped mace against his shield. "They won't take our pennon, will they Locke?"

Jurian took up the beat on his shield to match Turney's. "Nay, they will not." He laughed with Turney and moved forward.

The rest of the Red Team beat their shields in time. When the Blue Team joined them, the crowd's cheers were deafening. Above the roar of the crowd, a trumpet sounded, and the front line rushed forward into combat.

* * *

Elena listened to the catapult release another missile. From what she could observe, the trebuchet fired its smaller missiles much further, but the catapult threw the larger stones. She could see where the rocks met the ground east of the pavilion, but she could not watch the weapons fire due to the exuberance of the large man in front of her.

His page provided a steady supply of ale, and the man's unrestrained excitement blocked the field from view.

Perhaps he will soon leave in search of the privy.

A trumpet sang on the tournament field, and a cheer went up from the north pavilion. The excitement traveled around the tournament grounds and soon everyone around her came to their feet. Everyone but her.

She leaned as far as she could to her left to see a bit of the field.

Two lines of men wearing blue and red tunics stood before the King's pavilion.

"Your Majesty." The official's voice echoed from the field, but the rest was lost as the crowds clapped their hands and stamped their feet on the wooden planks.

"What's happening?" she asked the woman beside her, but her question went unheard or ignored.

Thump. Thump. Thump. The sound of drums, or of axes striking wood, reached the pavilion, but the roar from the crowd drowned the sound from the field.

"Please." She turned to the couple behind her. "What do you see?"

"The melee is beginning," a young man said to her.

He received an angry look from the woman beside him for his trouble.

Elena scooted as far as she could to the left. Half the field became visible as another trumpet sounded. The roar of the crowd alone thrilled her.

I wish I could stand without fear of falling.

To her right, another missile streaked fire across the sky, and a fireball exploded in the field. The war machine competition had reached its finale. Instead of stones, they fired small clay pots of burning pitch. The pots exploded upon impact but burned quickly to ash in the dirt field. By the distance, the last throw had been made by the catapult.

Another cheer went up for some action on the melee field. In the short silence that followed, the war machine commander called instructions to his men for the trebuchet. A whoosh and a clank sounded, and then the cries of excitement changed to screams of panic.

The trebuchet had misfired.

The large gentleman in front of her spun like a top, flames from burning pitch covered his face and torso. He tottered, and fell face down on the wooden floor. Flames licked along his backside and across the seat in front of her.

A sudden thrust from behind knocked her to the side. She threw herself away from the flame and tumbled backward off her bench directly into the path of those seeking to flee the fiery disaster. She covered her head as a man jumped over her. His female companion stepped on her in their rush to escape. Elena screamed in pain.

Above her, the awning burned. Bits of flaming material floated down on the terrified spectators as they fled the pavilion. Lying on the wooden board, she could see her crutch beneath her seat, outlined in flames, but she could not reach it.

Elena pushed herself to her knees. Most of the revelers in the pavilion had fled. Three people were down in the rows below her, and the flames advanced. She struggled to rise and crawl higher in the seats, away from the flame.

"Help me!" she begged the few remaining spectators as they fled. They didn't pause in their flight. She held her hand up to shield her face from the heat as the blaze inched toward her. Beyond the flames, people ran toward the pavilion, but they would never reach her in time.

CHAPTER FOUR

Jurian lifted the opponent before him with his shield and tossed the man onto another, knocking both off their feet. Beside him, Turney bellowed with laughter. The Red Team had moved forward, pushing the Blue Team across the middle of the field. He and Sir Turney halted any of the blue knights who tried to flank their main group.

"Forward!" Chessam yelled as he pounded at a blue-clad knight with his blunted axe. Blood ran from Chessam's nose, down his face, and into his mouth. It stained his teeth red and gave him a frightful visage as he grinned with mad glee.

Jurian and Turney fell back several paces as their team advanced toward their opponent's flag. Now would be the time for the Blue Team to launch a desperate attempt at the red flag.

A knight in a red tunic struggled up the earthen hill toward the prize—the blue pennon flying high from a wooden pole. Both teams fought fiercely at the base of the mound. Laughter and jesting had turned to serious competition as the end of the melee a pied drew near.

Jurian turned his head from side to side, watching for any blue knight who might try to rush their flag. A swift look to his left told him Turney guarded the back of the field as he did.

A sudden chill ran down Jurian's arms. The hair between the shortened hauberk and his leather gauntlets stood on end.

After such a long silence, Agaria calls me.

Nausea hit Jurian in the pit of his stomach as pain pierced between his eyes and shot through to the back of his skull. The shouts of men on the field grew distant and muted while a thin wail filled his ears. He shook his head and lifted his gaze to the blue flag atop the earthen hill. One of the men in red dove through the air and slowed to a halt. His hand, outstretched toward the blue pennon, frozen in midair.

Only a second had passed before time resumed, and the pennon disappeared beneath a pile of men who rolled down the hill. Jurian staggered backward, dropped his sword and shield, and dug the heels of his palms into his eyes.

The horrific pain inside his head narrowed to a stinging point at the back of his skull. He moved his head, and the prick of pain slid across his skin, never wavering in its direction.

Across the tournament field, flames had taken hold of the south pavilion. Spectators fled from both sides of the wood and cloth structure as fire rose from the center and licked at the awning.

The point of pain set directly between Jurian's eyes. He heard Turney yell, but Jurian's long strides had already taken him past the mound that held the red pennon.

At the south end of the tournament field, a curved five-foot earthen berm separated the melee from the war machines. Jurian vaulted to the top of the berm and skirted between the catapult and the broken trebuchet to reach the seats.

Pitch fires burned along the front of the pavilion and around the remains of the trebuchet. The firing teams had quickly fled the disaster. The tingling pain in his head remained between his eyes, but flames and smoke blocked his sight. He skirted a pile of burning pitch, grabbed the edge of the pavilion deck and pulled himself up and onto the risers.

The stinging point set over his right eye. He twisted his head to center the point between his brows.

She lay on the boards struggling to stand. Trapped beyond the flames. She appeared injured.

Jurian jumped through the wall of fire and reached for the girl, for his Agaria reborn.

Her head came up, and a stranger's gaze met his. Large brown eyes with blonde hair instead of black.

He recognized her intelligence—her soul—

behind those eyes. *My only love.*

"I can't stand," she called and choked as smoke rolled over them, along with the stench of burning flesh.

Jurian wrapped one arm around her waist and lifted her to his side. He covered her hair with his other hand, held her head close to his shoulder as he leapt through the flames, and down onto the war machine grounds.

He landed firm on both feet as pieces of the scorched awning floated down around the smoldering trebuchet. Blue and red knights from the melee had arrived, along with the water cart from the target field. Jurian paid them no mind. He shifted Agaria in his arms and carried her away as the stands caved in, and the whoosh of ash and sparks enveloped them.

When he reached the edge of the berm, he looked back at the burning pavilion with Agaria still clasped in his arms. "Are you injured?" His attention shifted to her face.

She smelled of smoke and ash, and that sweet, elusive scent all her own. She shook her head and coughed into his shoulder. "Nay." Her small trembling hand pushed against his chest. "You must put me down, please. I am well."

He lowered her legs to the ground, but instead of moving away from him, she clung to his arm. She held her slight weight on her left leg and leaned against his armored side.

"You *are* injured." His brows drew together, and he steadied her stance with his hand.

"Nay." She shook her head and blinked watering eyes. "I've no new injury, but an old one. I am well, Sir Knight." Her voice faded as she raised her gaze to his.

The point of pain between his eyes dissolved.

Her wide brown eyes spilled tears down pale smoke-stained cheeks, and she coughed.

His heart ached with the joy of reunion, and he swallowed the emotion building in his throat.

Oh, my eternal love.

Who had Agaria become? Whose daughter was she?

Whose wife?

* * *

Elena's blinked stinging smoke-drawn tears from her eyes and stared at the face of the man who saved her life. A chainmail coif covered his hair, but his brows were arched and dark. As dark as his eyes. His intense, intimate gaze thrilled a part of her she never knew existed.

Men never look at me like this.

She had observed this look on men's faces when they looked at her beautiful stepmother, but for her, their faces held disdain and pity, or at best,

31

friendship.

The King's pavilion had emptied onto the field and war machine area. Onlookers rushed to help the injured and douse the flames. Her knight shifted, and she swayed, clutching his arm to maintain her balance. "I beg your forgiveness, Sir," she choked an apology at her manners through a raw burning throat. Heat blossomed in her face, and she looked away from his penetrating gaze. "The old injury has left my leg lame. I cannot walk without my crutch."

Her knight presented his arm without a word, and she grasped it as she searched the chaotic field for her father's green cloak or Heloise's bright headpiece.

They will think I perished in the blaze.

"Locke!" Two unarmored men hurried to where they stood. The older man she recognized as Sir Albert Clavel, their neighbor in Essex and suitor for her hand. The younger man, Sir Albert's former squire Sir Reginald Vale.

She glanced up at her knight. *Sir Locke?*

The two men came to a halt, and their attention shifted from her tall savior to her.

"Lady Gregory." Sir Clavel dipped his head. "Are you injured?"

Elena shook her head and gripped her knight's arm tighter. "Nay, I am well." Her regard went from Clavel to the towering man beside her. "I was trapped, and somehow he found me."

"Elena?" The Earl of Hawthorn rushed across the field calling her name. "Elena?"

The sound of her father's desperate voice sent a pulse of emotion through her chest. She waved her free arm to get his attention. "Father—I am here."

His silver-grey head and green cloak came towards her through the crowd. When he reached her, he lifted her into his arms and held her close, his voice choking with relief. "I saw the fire, and I knew I couldn't reach you in time. My dear, Elena, I thought I'd lost you."

"She's safe." Heloise followed Warner to the small group and laid her palm on her husband's shoulder. "Praise our Father in Heaven for this miracle—Elena is safe." With her other hand on her chest, she gasped for breath. "We were in the King's pavilion when the trebuchet misfired." She shook her head and pointed at the smoldering pavilion. "The burning pot flew into the seats right where we left Elena."

"I fell backward when the crowd ran and became trapped between the seats," Elena told Heloise as Warner set Elena back on her feet. She held her father's arm for balance. With her other arm, she reached toward her knight. "This man came through the flames to save me." She shook her head. "I shall never know how you found me."

"I don't believe I know your name, Sir, but you have my profound thanks." The Earl bowed his head to Jurian.

"Lord Gregory." Sir Albert Clavel indicated Jurian. "This brave man is Jurian Locke. He and I met on the road to London not a fortnight ago, under less than pleasant circumstances. He came to our defense when we were set upon by thieves. Sir Reginald took a wound from those brigands. Locke agreed to champion the Clavel Banner in the tournament."

Albert addressed Jurian. "Jurian, may I present His Lordship, Warner Gregory, Earl of Hawthorn, his daughter, Lady Elena, and his wife, Lady Heloise."

Jurian's eyebrows rose, and his gaze flicked to Elena, and then back to her father as he bowed. "It is my honor to make your acquaintance, My Lord."

"I am forever in your debt, Sir Locke." The Earl handed support of Elena to his wife.

"Unfortunately, I am no sir, nor a knight. A simple man-at-arms, My Lord." When Jurian lifted his head, his eyes met Elena's.

Heloise slipped beneath Elena's arm with a hand around her waist.

Elena bounced on her good leg to maintain balance as she craned her neck to stare at Jurian Locke.

Not a knight?

The smoke from the pavilion changed from black to white as the fire was extinguished. The field emptied of spectators as they returned to their seats in the King's pavilion.

Trumpets sounded while the few injured were taken from the field for treatment. Ushers in King's livery strung bright pennon banners to separate areas for individual combat. The tournament would continue despite the fiery disaster.

"We must return to the pavilion. King Edward has offered us seats near His Highness to watch the individual tournaments and jousting." The Earl gave Jurian a brief nod. "Again, Locke, you have my gratitude and my debt."

"Not at all." Jurian bowed in return, his gaze slipping between father and daughter.

Elena cast one more look over her shoulder at Jurian, and then her father walked beside her, helping Heloise steady his daughter.

"He certainly is a tall man," Heloise said to her husband.

Warner nodded. "And fast. It was he who I saw race across the field as the fire started."

"It was as though he knew where I fell," Elena murmured.

They reached the pavilion stairs, but Heloise tipped her head toward the ladies tent. "Elena needs to wash the ash from her face before she greets the King, Warner. We'll be only a moment."

Her father nodded and waited by the steps.

Inside the tent, several of the women who had

been in the south pavilion were washing and repinning their hair. Maids provided soft damp cloths to bathe their face and hands.

Elena accepted a cool, damp cloth and covered her face, but Heloise took the material and wiped the ash from her brow.

"Did you see him, Heloise? He picked me up with one arm and carried me from the fire."

Heloise nodded and scrubbed at a spot on Elena's cheek. "Yes, he's impossible to miss. The man is as tall as the giants of old."

"I think he's handsome. Do you find him handsome?" Elena took the cloth from Heloise and held it to her eyes. They still burned from the smoke.

"Well-favored enough, I suppose, for a young girl to be quite taken with her rescuer." Heloise pressed her lips. "However, let me remind you that your father hoped to make a match that will benefit us all. Sir Clavel has land that adjoins ours. Piers Ramsey will inherit his father's estate." Heloise shook her head. "This man, this Jurian Locke, is but a man-at-arms. Not a knight and not landed I'd wager."

Elena's grin faded, and she handed the maid the damp cloth. "I know." She took Heloise's arm. "Besides, what brave and handsome man would find loveliness here? Surely a man as gallant and brave as Jurian Locke could seek a fairer maid."

Heloise clucked her tongue as they ducked through the tent opening. "A fairer maid could never be found, my dear. Besides, that brave and gallant man ran through fire to save you." She smiled at Elena as they paused before the steps. "Perhaps such a chivalrous deed will obtain recognition."

"Oh good." Warner turned to his wife and daughter. "We have been summoned to speak with King Edward."

CHAPTER FIVE

Heloise and Warner helped Elena up the steps of the King's pavilion and assisted her through the crowded stands toward the royal enclosure. Resplendent with rich tapestries and high-backed cushioned chairs, King Edward, and his young wife, Philippa, sat in the center of the dais. The king's mother, Isabella, Roger Mortimer, the Earl of March, and Henry, the Earl of Lancaster sat in cushioned chairs on a riser behind the young sovereign and his bride.

Elena's eyebrows rose as the king faced her. *King Edward is no older than I.*

She held tight to her father's arm while she curtsied. "Your Majesty."

"Are you the girl the knight carried from the fire?" Edward asked, sitting forward.

At a loss for words, Elena could only murmur, "Yes, Your Majesty."

"That was the bravest thing I've ever witnessed." King Edward glanced at his wife, then back to Elena. "Philippa had just prayed everyone escaped when we saw a man leap through the blaze and onto the field with you in his arms." He gestured to the area where the individual combat competitions were beginning. "You must tell me his name so we may cheer him in the joust."

Elena looked uneasily at her father.

"The brave man's name is Jurian Locke, Your Majesty," her father responded in her stead. "We only discovered that ourselves when we found him on the field with Elena." Her father placed his warm hand over hers. "Unfortunately, his name will not appear on the lists. He is only a man-at-arms and may not participate in the joust."

Edward turned to his mother. "Is this true?"

The Queen Dowager tipped her head in assent. "It is. Only the bravest champions of the realm may participate in the joust to win the tournament."

Edward shook his head. "If that be the case, then this man would surely qualify. What greater bravery have we beheld this day or any other?"

"Yet he must be knighted to joust," Roger Mortimer, the Earl of March, advised the king. "It is, of course, understandable that such a display of bravery would earn this man his knighthood."

"Then he shall be knighted." King Edward addressed Henry, the Earl of Lancaster, who sat on the other side of his mother from Mortimer. "How should we proceed?"

The Earl of Lancaster leaned toward Warner, his

elbow on his knee. "Is Locke your man?"

Warner bowed his head as he spoke to the Regent. "Nay. He carries Sir Albert Clavel's banner, My Lord."

The Earl of Lancaster switched his regard to the young king. "Your Majesty, I recommend his patron, Sir Albert Clavel, present his spurs and take his Oath of Knighthood on the field before the joust. There is a natural break before the joust. A knighting would please the crowd while they reset the field for the last event." Henry raised a brow at Warner. "I'd wager the Earl of Hawthorn will vouch as the man's second patron. Locke may complete his knighthood ritual after the games, by your leave, Your Grace."

"Done." King Edward motioned for his attendant. "Have Sir Jurian Locke's name added to the lists and send a page to Sir Albert Clavel informing him of the ceremony. Provide Sir Clavel with all he needs for the knighting." King Edward waved his hand, and one of the attendants bowed and disappeared from the dais.

Edward returned his attention to the tournaments. He pointed toward the Swordsman's Competition and spoke softly to Philippa.

The Queen Dowager gestured to the attendant at her shoulder. "Please find seats for the Earl of Hawthorn and his family." She tipped her head at Warner and Elena, and they were dismissed.

Warner helped his daughter back from the dais and followed the attendant toward the north end of the pavilion. They moved down the risers to the front of the stands.

"Make room, make room." The attendant waved his arms, and the spectators shifted tighter, creating seats for Elena and her parents. The servant bowed to her father. "Will there be anything else, My Lord?"

"Could a merchant be summoned with ale and wine?" Warner asked the man. "I hesitate to leave my daughter again."

"Yes, My Lord. I'll send one to attend you." The servant bowed and disappeared up the steps.

"Are you sure you're well?" Heloise leaned forward and whispered across her husband to Elena. "You're still very pale."

"Do you feel ill?" her father inquired.

Elena shook head, but her thoughts continued to whirl. This disorientation had to be the speed at which events had befallen. For the first time that she could remember, she wanted a man to look at her again the way Jurian Locke had when he held her in his arms.

My knight. Sir Jurian Locke

* * *

In the north pavilion, Milton Ramsey made his

way down the aisle and took the seat beside his son, Piers. Milton handed his son a tankard of ale. "You were right. The woman carried from the flames was indeed Elena Gregory." He glared at his son.

How could this virile young man not win the hand of the Earl's crippled daughter?

"I thought so. I recognized the color of her gown. Elena always favors blue." Piers took a drink of the ale. "She's fortunate that man found her. She would not have made it from the pavilion by herself with her crutch.

Milton took a swig of ale and leaned closer to his son. "I diverted behind the royal dais as I returned from the ale merchant. The Earl of Hawthorn had an audience with the king." Milton wiped the foam from his mustache. "It appears Sir Clavel hired a man-at-arms to take Sir Reginald Vale's place in the tournament after Vale's unfortunate injury on the road."

"Sir Reginald is injured?" Piers eyebrows rose as he looked at his father.

"More than that, it's the very same man-at-arms who saved Elena from the flames."

Piers shook his head. "Such strange fortune. I had no idea." He gestured to the field. "I saw the Clavel shield in the melee, and I assumed…"

Milton turned with disgust from his son. "You assumed wrong, as usual."

Perhaps if Piers were a knight, the Gregory girl

might favor him.

The Earl's daughter had few suitors. Even with an Earldom attached to the lame chit, takers were few. Who wanted a feeble son born from a crippled mother? But the choice between an elderly knight and his handsome son should be no choice at all. And yet the girl hesitated, and her father gave in to her wishes.

Chastised, Piers took another draw from his ale and stared at the field in silence.

Milton frowned at his son. Both he and Clavel were land owners whose property adjoined the Hawthorn estate.

The Earl should force his daughter's hand.

His precious child didn't need to love his son. They had played together as children and knew each other well.

I don't understand why she withholds her affection.

Too bad old Albert survived the ambush; then the choice would have been taken from her hands.

The king had let it be known that the Tournament Champion could ask a boon, in addition to the substantial number of purses the champion would amass by winning the most events. The knight with the most wins would be proclaimed the Christmas Tournament Champion.

Milton had taken Sir Sedrick Hollander into his service precisely to win the championship and earn a boon from the king. Sir Sedrick had won a reputation as a fine jouster. His plan and Clavel's were the same. Win a boon from the king and force the Earl of Hawthorn's hand regarding his crippled child.

As luck would have it, Sir Sedrick's Blue Team lost the melee a pied tournament. Then Clavel's man-at-arms won the archery contest Sir Sedrick had declined to enter. Sir Sedrick told Milton a knight had neither the time nor the need to sharpen his skill at archery. Only two events remained—the Swordsman's Competition and the Joust. Both competitions were highly regarded and therefore earned the most tournament points.

His son sat up and pointed at the field. "They've reached the final for the Swordsman's Competition. Sir Clavel's pennon stands beside the ring."

"Yes, and he meets our Sir Sedrick." Milton sat forward in his seat. "Clavel's man is an archer, not a knight. Sir Sedrick should make an easy meal of this Jurian Locke."

* * *

Jurian ran his arms through the leather straps and lifted the small buckler from Maury's hands.

"You still need plate for the joust." Reginald leaned against the gate, surveying Jurian's armor. "This piecemeal attire is fine for the small games.

At least we found gauntlets and a helmet, though I don't know where we'll find a breastplate with a lance rest in your size."

"They refused to add my name to the lists. There is no need for plate." Jurian took the blunted sword Maury held and advanced. "The Swordsman's Competition will be my last game today." He shrugged at Reginald. "I haven't seen Sir Albert since I was refused the list. He doesn't know."

Reginald nodded. "With your wins on the field so far, even second place on the joust would have taken the championship."

A trumpet sounded, and the herald announced the next match. "Sir Sedrick Hollander for House Ramsey shall meet Jurian Locke for House Clavel."

"He wears unnecessary armor," Reginald noted as they walked toward the swordsman's ring.

"It will make him slow." Jurian grinned at Reginald and crossed the dirt field to the herald.

The two swordsmen met beside the herald.

"This competition will determine the Champion of the Sword. You both know the rules—disarm your opponent two times or three unanswered tags win the bout." The herald looked at both men and waited for their nod of understanding.

Jurian tapped Sir Sedrick's outstretched sword, and both men stepped back. The herald ducked under the stringer of colorful pennons that marked the competition boundary and marched toward the pavilion to announce the final match.

CHAPTER SIX

Elena gripped her father's forearm and pointed toward the Swordsman's Competition. "There's Jurian."

Warner nodded. "He faces the Ramsey Knight." He leaned toward his wife. "The irony here abounds."

Heloise covered her mouth and giggled. "For whom do you cheer, husband?"

"Why, the chivalrous soon-to-be knight that saved my daughter's life, of course." He grinned at the grip Elena had on his jacket. "The swords are blunted, my dear. No grave harm should come to either man."

Elena bit her nail. Her heart beat in her throat, and she swallowed as she nodded to her father. "I know."

The field in front of the King's pavilion had been cleared of spectators by the heralds before the competition. No one would be allowed to impede the royal perspective of the Swordsman's Competition. This gave Elena a clear view of the match as well.

The trumpets sounded, and the Herald of the Field moved forward. "Your Majesty, may I present Sir Sedrick Hollander for House Ramsey, and Jurian Locke for House Clavel. This is the final match for the Swordsman's Competition. The winner will be proclaimed the Champion of the Sword, receive the winner's purse, and be awarded tournament points."

King Edward nodded.

The herald signaled the judges who held small flags on either side of the ring and would signal when a point had been struck.

The trumpet sounded again, and the match commenced.

Taller by two hands, Jurian remained in his chainmail and leather armor, while Sir Sedrick wore a plated gorget around his neck and spaulders to protect his shoulders.

Jurian should have such armor.

Elena chewed across from one nail to the next.

The clash of the dulled blades rang across the field as the combatants engaged. Sir Sedrick attacked first and rained a flurry of high blows at his opponent's head.

Jurian blocked each strike and retaliated with a similar set of movements. The men separated and paced the circle, gauging each other.

Jurian danced forward struck an overhand blow

against Sedrick's sword, then lifted his shield to Sedrick's blade and slapped the flat of his sword against Sedrick's hip.

A cheer went up in the pavilions, along with the flag held by the judge.

"Point to Clavel," announced the herald.

Sedrick surged forward, throwing blow after blow at Jurian's head and shield, unable to find an opening in his opponent's defense.

As Sedrick moved back, Jurian advanced, giving Sedrick no time to set a defense. Using the same technique as before, Jurian pushed his opponent's sword to the side with his buckler and scored a hit against the knight's hip.

The flag rose again, and the spectators in the pavilion stamped their feet in anticipation of a quick victory.

"A second point to Clavel."

Both Elena's father and the man beside her rose to their feet cheering. Elena didn't look away from the field to notice if her step-mother stood. Elena couldn't tear her gaze from Jurian. She shifted to the front of her seat, as much as she possible, and cheered for her knight until her throat became raw.

Sir Sedrick jumped back and swung his sword through the air in a display of prowess, then pounded the metal against his buckler as he advanced.

Jurian skirted sideways and lunged, but Sedrick

blocked his attempt, moved forward and swung his sword not at Jurian's body or shield, but at his sword hand. The edge of Sedrick's dulled blade clipped the back of Jurian's hand, and Jurian's weapon flew from his numbed fingers.

The flag went up, and the herald strode into the ring to separate the fighters while Jurian retrieved his sword.

"Point to Ramsey," the herald bellowed.

"What is Jurian doing?" Elena tugged her father's coat. "Why did he take up his shield with his other hand?"

Warner resumed his seat and leaned toward Elena. "That strike must have injured his sword hand. He intends to fight with his left hand."

"That's not fair. The other knight injured him on purpose." Elena's face burned with outrage. "I could see that from here." She held out her hand toward the field as in evidence of the misdeed.

The crowd hissed to show their displeasure at Sir Sedrick's churlish act.

The herald left the ring, and the fighters advanced.

The end of the match came quickly as Sir Sedrick tangled their swords and then butted Jurian with his buckler as he stripped the sword from his hand.

* * *

Sir Sedrick's hard slam from his buckler knocked the hilt of his sword from Jurian's hand. He had lost the match. Jurian backed away and bowed.

Sir Sedrick mirrored Jurian's bow with a broad grin on his face.

The herald escorted Sir Sedrick across the field to stand before the King's pavilion. "Your Majesty, I present the Champion of the Sword, Sir Sedrick Hollander, representing House Ramsey." From his vest, the herald withdrew a small bag of coins. "Congratulations, Sir." He handed the pouch to Sir Sedrick, bowed and moved away.

Sir Sedrick raised his buckler and sword to the crowd in victory, first to the King's pavilion, and then to the north stands. The crowd cheered the champion louder this time.

Jurian picked up his tournament sword and left the combat area. He caught sight of Elena's blue gown near the front of the King's pavilion and hesitated. His desire to approach her almost overwhelmed his good sense. Instead, he shook his head and headed for the Clavel tent.

Best wait until the feast tonight.

Sir Reginald and Sir Albert spoke near the edge of the tournament field. Reginald held *Baraca* in one hand, and a white robe draped over his arm. Sir Albert wore his polished chainmail beneath a blue and gold tunic that displayed his coat of arms. The old knight's face beamed with pride.

Jurian looked from Reginald's broad grin to Albert's smiling face. "You do know I lost the competition?"

"I care not for the Swordsman's crown," Sir Albert declared. "I have great news, and we have very little time to prepare." He approached Jurian with silver spurs clasped in his hand. "King Edward sent an attendant to me with instructions for a knighting. *Your* knighting."

"Mine?" Jurian shook his head. *How shall I swear an oath when bonded to my love?*

Albert nodded. "You shall be knighted, as though upon the field of battle, and ride in the jousting final, by order of the king."

"Why? How did this come about?"

Reginald took the tournament sword from Jurian's hand and dropped it into a barrel of swords. "You'll not need that." Reginald handed *Baraca* to Albert as Maury raced up with damp cloths. "Ah Maury, good speed. Give the towel to Locke." He spun the robe in his hand and opened the bottom of the skirt, preparing to fit the cloth over Jurian's head. "Remove the filth of battle from your face and hands, Jurian. You must be draped in this white robe for the knighting."

Jurian returned the towels to Maury and allowed Reginald to drop the white tunic over his head and adjust the cloth belt. "I must know the oath before I swear it." He gripped Albert's arm. "A bond already weighs upon my soul that I cannot forsake. I do not wish to swear an oath to you, or to the king, that I cannot hold sacred."

Albert's brows rose nearly to his hairline. "You swore an oath to another?"

"I swore no oath. How the bond came about is a tale for another time. What I must know are the Vows and Oaths of Knighthood that you would have me swear this day."

Albert nodded, took Jurian's arm and walked toward the tournament field. "I shall ask you to swear allegiance to me as your Lord. You will repeat the Oath of Knighthood as I speak it to you."

They skirted the field attendants who collected the streaming banner from the sword competition and moved away from the preparation for the joust in front of the King's pavilion.

As they approached the herald, who waited in the middle of the field, Albert's voice became softer and rushed. "You shall never deal with traitors. You shall defend the weak, the orphan, the widow and the oppressed to your utmost ability. You must treat all women with great respect and defend them, whether they are married or not, against all. Lastly, you must swear to observe fasts, abstinences, hear Mass, and make an offering to the Church. Can you swear to this?"

Jurian and Albert stopped near the herald, and Jurian nodded. "Yes. I find no compromise between these oaths and my bond.

"Are you ready to proceed?" the herald asked.

Sir Albert nodded and faced Jurian.

The herald approached the King's pavilion, stopped and bowed to the king. "Your Majesty, by your decree, may I present the Knighting of Jurian Locke, for his chivalrous bravery on the field this day."

* * *

Everyone in the pavilion rose to their feet as Jurian knelt in the field.

Elena's father helped her stand and placed his arm around her shoulders.

"I can't hear what they're saying," Elena whispered to her father.

Warner leaned close to his daughter's head. "He's swearing the Oath of Knighthood; to always be honest and brave, to respect all women, and observe the Church's holy days."

Sir Albert drew a sword from its scabbard and held the hilt, which formed a cross, toward Jurian. They spoke for several moments, then Albert grasped the sword by the hilt and laid the flat blade on Jurian's shoulder—raised the blade—and laid it on the other shoulder.

Jurian rose from his knees, towering over Sir Albert, and the old knight strapped the sword around Jurian's white robe and handed him his spurs.

The herald faced the King's pavilion. "Your Majesty, may I present to you Sir Jurian Locke, sworn in oath to the House Clavel and your service."

The cheers from the crowd were deafening.

Warner steadied Elena as she bounced on her good foot and cheered for her knight.

When the roar of the crowd faded, they took their seats and looked at the new area cordoned off on the field. Ten paces in front of the King's pavilion the jousting run had been erected. Two sides, divided by strings of colorful pennons.

Men and horses gathered at both ends of the run.

CHAPTER SEVEN

Sir Albert paced the Clavel tent. "Where is Maury? He should have returned by now."

Sir Reginald, acting as the squire, helped Jurian into the heavy padded undershirt he would wear beneath his breastplate and tightened the laces on one side.

Cheers from the spectators echoed in the chill afternoon air.

"Tell me again why I need not compete on the field except against the winner?" Jurian turned and lifted his arm for Reginald to secure the other side. "How can this be a competition if I face only the last man?"

Albert returned from the tent opening. "One reason is you have yet to obtain your armor." He picked up a tankard of ale from the table. "King Edward ordered his attendant to help Maury find pieces ample enough for your devilishly large frame." Albert took a swig of ale. "By the Gods, you're a big man."

Reginald bade Jurian sit and removed his leather footwear. "You shall be deemed the Patchwork Knight, without a doubt. None of the pieces Maury has found are similar in style, color, nor strength."

His gaze met Jurian's and he laughed. "You shall be a quite a tremendous sight."

Jurian smiled. "I care not about the appearance of my armor. It troubles me I did not compete to win my place in the final. I cannot help but think this unfair to the other knights who have jousted days for a chance to compete today."

Reginald sat back on his heels and shook his head at Jurian. "None of these men were knighted on the field today. Your place in the list is by the king's command. The other men understand this recognition from the king, even if you do not." He held up the chainmail skirt. "Take this and let us dress you in what we have."

Jurian stepped into the armor and pulled the metal skirt to his hips.

Reginald adjusted and strapped the armor in place, then proceed to arm Jurian's legs.

"We need only a jouster's breastplate and a helm." Albert peeked from the tent. "Ah, here comes Maury. He's found the rest."

Albert held the flap wide as Maury struggled in with the heavy chest armor. Behind him came the royal attendant carrying a helmet.

"I think this will fit, Sir." Maury set the armor next to Reginald. "It's the biggest we could find."

"The king sends his greetings. He has offered to make partial recompense for the purchase of this armor." The attendant bowed to Albert. "King

Edward knows this armor comes as an unexpected expense for the patrons."

"You purchased this armor?" Jurian ducked into the breastplate as Reginald and Maury tightened and adjusted the leather straps. "I mistakenly believed they were loaned to us."

"The cost is divided between the patrons." Albert picked up a gauntlet and waited while Reginald adjusted the gorget and pauldrons.

"How many patrons do I have?" Jurian slipped one hand into the gauntlet Maury held and the other into the gauntlet Albert offered.

"Two, not including the king. The Earl of Hawthorn and myself." Albert shook his head at Jurian and grinned. "There shall be no mistaking you."

Jurian took stock of his costume. A plain black breastplate above a chainmail skirt. The greaves along his shins were plain silver, while his shoulder pauldrons were dark and finely etched with delicate scroll work. The gorget around his neck had a rose tint and engraved with filigree. The helmet in the attendant's hand was plain, without the usual decorative top feathers, for which Jurian was thankful.

A patchwork knight indeed.

The royal attendant handed Jurian the helm. "I shall inform the king our newest knight is prepared to enter the field." The attendant bowed and left the tent with a merry grin and a twinkle in his eye.

Jurian shook his head. "Even the servants laughs at my armor." He slid the helmet over his head and lifted the visor.

"Is Zeus ready?" Albert asked as he left the tent.

"Aye," Reginald replied and followed Jurian out of the opening.

Jurian stopped outside the tent as a sudden cheer went up around him. A dozen knights who had fought with him in the melee, or competed against him in the archery and swordsman's competitions waited outside the Clavel tent for him to appear.

Maury ran around the side of the tent and coaxed Zeus forward. The destrier had been draped in a full closure of blue and gold, the Clavel colors.

Jurian swore the big horse lifted his front hooves in a prance.

Reginald took Zeus's bit as Albert assisted Jurian onto the saddle.

Maury handed Albert the Clavel jousting shield, then ran back for the lances.

"Be careful," Albert told Jurian as he handed up the shield.

"Be careful, you say?" Jurian laughed. "You never even asked if I could joust."

Albert's mouth dropped open, and he glanced from Jurian to Reginald and back. "Can you not?"

"Well enough to remain alive, though barely. I do not promise to win." Jurian urged Zeus forward, and they rode through the crowded tent area.

"But you must," Albert called. "I must have my boon!"

The king's boon.

How could Jurian have forgotten Sir Albert's desire to marry Elena? Finding and saving his beloved in her new life never guaranteed she would return his affection. And yet, he hoped that Elena might.

Zeus carried him through the tent village and onto the field.

Elena need not return my affection for me to love and care for her.

He would be at her side, serving her and Sir Albert.

I would keep both Elena and Sir Albert safe.

He ground his teeth at the bitter pill his station in life gave him. An unlanded knight could never hope to wed the daughter of an Earl.

The screams and cheers from the crowd pulled Jurian from his thoughts.

The field official approached Zeus cautiously and waited for Jurian to turn the horse to the side. "This is the last run between Sir Sedrick Hollander and Sir Davis Fowler. The score is one, one.

The crack of a lance and the gasp of the crowd cause both men to look up. Cheers erupted as Sir Davis climbed to his feet from the dirt.

"The victor of this bout is Sir Sedrick

Hollander," the herald announced to the King's pavilion.

"You've been matched against Sir Sedrick before," the field official noted with a grin.

"Aye," Jurian said. "I know the man. He plays fair just this side of foul."

"Keep that in mind on your runs." The official nodded. "Best of luck, Sir Jurian." The liveried official indicated the far end of the jousting field.

Jurian urged Zeus forward, and the cheers grew louder. Zeus nodded his head and pranced across the field. Jurian grinned at the horse's antics. "For an old destrier, you certainly relish the applause." He reached the end of the run and turned to face the track. Across the field followed Maury and Sir Reginald, carrying his lances.

They rested two of the lances in a curved stand nearby. Maury waited by the stand as Reginald approached and handed Jurian his jouster's pole. "It *would* be Sedrick you meet. He's poised to win the tournament if he unseats you."

"It is the best two of three runs. Don't count me out, Reggie. I'm no novice at this game."

Reginald gaped at Jurian. "You led Albert to believe you could barely sit a horse, much less handle a lance."

Jurian chuckled. "I didn't want Albert to think this an easy win." Jurian nodded across the field where Sir Sedrick took up a new lance and spoke to his squire. "He's an accomplished knight."

"He plays loose with the rules."

"I shall be watchful."

Trumpets sounded, and the Herald moved forward. "Your Majesty, I now present to you the final Jousting match of the Christmas Tournament—the Chevalier match between Sir Sedrick Hollander and Sir Jurian Locke. The winner of this contest will receive enough tournament points to be proclaimed the Champion of the Tournament." The herald threw up his hands and bowed over his leg. He rose as trumpets sounded the beginning of the contest.

* * *

Elena cheered as Jurian rode the huge white horse onto the field. "Is that Sir Albert's horse? Why is Sir Jurian's armor so diverse?"

Warner laughed. "Yes, that is Sir Albert's destrier, and your knight is too big to fit a regular sized man's armor."

The herald announced the match.

Jurian took up his lance and rode the white animal toward the jousting run.

"What is he doing?" She glanced at her father, then back at Jurian.

The horse pranced past the jousting run and toward their seats.

"He's going to ask for your favor," Heloise whispered behind her husband's back. "I tied your extra ribbons to your cane."

"But my crutch burned in the fire."

Jurian slowed his pace as he approached the seats.

When the crowd understood his intention they their stamped their feet and cheered.

"Quick, let me pull a ribbon from your hair." With agile fingers, Heloise untied two red ribbons from Elena's long braid.

Unable to stand, she held up the ribbons and waited until Jurian held the tip of the lance to her.

Elena tied the ribbons around the lance amid the cheers from the crowd, and then sat back as Jurian lifted her ribbons like a trophy. The silken red ribbons fluttered in the wind.

"My Lady," he said to her as he bowed his head. He turned the horse and cantered back to the jousting run.

Elena covered her mouth with her hand as she caught her breath in a sob. Never had she dreamed a knight would show her such honor. She faced her father as tears rimmed her eyes and slid down her cheeks.

"Oh, my dear. Why do you cry?" He put his arm around her and glanced at Heloise

Tears sparkled on his wife's face as well.

He wrapped his other arm around Heloise.

"Enough tears, my darlings. You must find your voice to cheer Elena's knight. I fear he will need all our best wishes and prayers to win this competition."

* * *

Jurian closed his visor, rested the lance on the lance-hook beneath his right arm, and slid his gauntlet down the shaft to the vamplate. Elena's ribbons fluttered before him in the chill breeze. Several snowflakes blew past the front of his visor. The metal armor chilled his skin. He aimed the blunted tip at Sir Sedrick and waited for the trumpet.

The lances were hollow, designed to shatter upon direct impact with his opponent's shield. A shattered lance scored a point as did unseating his opponent. The knight who earned the most points after three runs would claim the victory.

Zeus tensed between his legs, anxious to run. The destrier knew this game and was eager to play. The trumpet sounded a charge and Zeus dug his hooves into the field and leapt forward without urging.

Jurian leaned headlong, keeping his eye on Sedrick's shield. Too far to the side and the lance would skip off, only a center hit would shatter his pole.

As the lancers met, Jurian's strike came a moment too late, and Sir Sedrick's lance shattered against Jurian's shield.

The horses continued to the end of the run, where both men acquired a new lance.

"First point to Sir Sedrick Hollander of House Ramsey."

Jurian braced the lance beneath his arm. He'd made a foolish error and should have struck harder at the moment of impact.

I'll not make that mistake again. I must win, for Elena.

A blast from the trumpet and Zeus surge forward. This time, as the lancers engaged, Jurian thrust his chest and lance forward into the Sir Sedrick's shield. Splinters flew past his visor as he finished the run. When Zeus turned, Sedrick held an unbroken lance.

"Second point to Sir Jurian Locke of House Clavel."

Reginald handed him a new lance. "Be alert this time. He'll angle for the inside of your shield."

Jurian nodded as the trumpet called.

Zeus galloped down the course toward Sedrick. Jurian aimed his lance at the center of his opponent's shield.

As Reginald predicted, the tip of Sedrick's lance moved toward Jurian's body.

When they engaged, Jurian angled his shield

away from his chest, forcing the tip of Sedrick's lance to slide away from Jurian's chest. At the same time, he leaned forward and thrust his lance into the center of Sedrick's shield.

Jurian's lance bowed for a moment, then shattered as he and Zeus sped past Sir Sedrick. When they turned at the end of the run, he discovered two field officials assisting Sir Sedrick to his feet. Jurian handed his shattered lance to an attendant. "Is Sir Sedrick injured?"

The attendant shook his head. "I doubt it. He lost his balance after you passed. He took no harm from your lance."

"The third and winning point is awarded to Sir Jurian Locke and House Clavel."

Jurian pulled the helmet from his head and tossed it to an attendant. "Gods, but I hate to joust."

Maury ran to the attendant, breathless, and pulled the helmet from his hands. "I'll take that."

Jurian smiled an apology at the man and held out is hand to Maury. "Take the gauntlets."

Maury pulled one gauntlet from Jurian's hand and set it beside the helmet. He gave the field attendant a suspicious glare. "They want you in front of the pavilion." He pulled off the second gauntlet and set it beside the first. "I'll watch your armor."

Threads of color caught Jurian's eye and he pointed toward the ground. "Maury, untangle those ribbons from the lance and tie them around my arm."

Maury untangled the ribbons and reached up to tie the colors around Jurian's armor, just above the elbow. "You should go. The herald is calling for you."

"My thanks, Maury." With a wink and a grin, Jurian tugged the reins and Zeus pranced proudly onto the field before the pavilion. As horse and rider separated from the crowd of men at the end of the jousting run, spectators split the air in sounds of favor for their new champion.

Jurian waved to the crowd, but his attention was captured by a blue dress. As the destrier passed Elena's seat, Jurian nodded and his gaze caught hers.

Agaria's inner beauty glimmered through Elena's dark eyes.

He reined Zeus near the herald and turned the magnificent horse to face King Edward.

"Your Majesty, may I present the Christmas Tournament Champion, Sir Jurian Locke for House Clavel."

Jurian bowed his head to the young king, while the herald folded low over his outstretched leg.

King Edward rose and looked down from his dais in the pavilion. "Congratulations, Sir Locke on your victory today. Your gallant bravery and triumphant feats in this last game before Lent have shown us the true spirit of our chivalrous knights.

"It is our wish that you feast with us tonight in celebration of our savior's birth and this joyous season. This eve we shall discuss the true prize you have won at this tournament." King Edward gestured to the herald and resumed his seat beside the young queen.

The herald handed Jurian an evergreen garland, decorated with mistletoe and silver ribbons, along with a hefty bag of coins.

Thankful the big horse behaved and didn't mistake the herald for a snack; Jurian lifted the festive garland into the air, and the crowd broke into cries of delight. "I am humbled by this honor." He nodded to the herald, then pulled the reins. Zeus pranced along the pavilion to the front of Elena's seat.

Her father helped Elena step to the edge of the stands in front of Jurian and Zeus.

Jurian handed the Earl of Hawthorn the evergreen garland, who then laid the braid of fragrant pine in Elena's arms. "My Lady." Jurian bowed his head as the eager crowd came to their feet one last time.

"Until tonight," Elena called to him as the cheering died down.

Jurian dipped his head to her and her father, and then reined Zeus and rode across the field to where Maury and Reginald waited.

CHAPTER EIGHT

Decorated for the joyous season, the King's palace at Westminster echoed the colors of the Earl of Hawthorn's coat of arms. Red and green on a field of white. The late afternoon flurries increased, leaving a soft layer of snow on the ground.

The Earl took his ladies home to his London manor to change for the feast and celebration. Kelsey accompanied Elena on their return, as both a maid and companion, leaving her father and step-mother to enjoy the evening without worry over her sake. Elena walked with her new cane through the entry and across the foyer to the large hall. Fires blazed in the massive hearths, warding the chill from the room.

At the far end of the large room, a raised dais held six chairs. Tables lined each side of the hall forming a large U-shape, leaving the wide floor between for minstrels, carolers, and tumblers.

There would be dancing after the meal, and Elena resigned herself to watching from the sidelines, although this eve she could at least see her knight move across the dance floor.

I will enjoy watching Sir Jurian dance.

A coat attendant had taken their outer garments when they entered the foyer. At the hall entrance, a seating usher spoke quietly to her father, nodded and then led the way into the room, winding through the throng of royal guests.

"We are seated on the far side, close to the dais," Warner informed Heloise and Elena as he rounded the table. "We are honored this evening, in appreciation of your knight." Warner grinned at his daughter.

Elena and Kelsey followed the Earl and his wife down the length of the table. "When I'm seated, find yourself a bit of dinner," Elena whispered to Kelsey. "I worry you will stand service through my seven-course meal while starving."

Kelsey grinned at her mistress and nodded. "Once you're seated, I shall."

Kelsey hurried from the room as soon as Elena assured her she was comfortable.

Concern for Kelsey's supper fled from her head as her knight entered the hall. Flanked by Sir Albert and Sir Reginald, Sir Jurian's gaze found hers immediately. Her breath caught as a smile lifted his face and brightened his eyes. She dropped her sight to her plate as her cheeks burned.

Fie, it is unfair. If only...

Aware Jurian approached, she cast a quick look

toward him.

He wore tall leather boots, charcoal-colored chausses and a long dark surcoat that covered his braies. With no head covering, his close-trimmed hair stood in stark contrast to the other men's long locks in the room. But her knight was like no one else.

"My Lady," he murmured as he paused near her chair and bowed.

So much emotion filled his eyes as he looked at her.

Why?

And what did she feel? Certainly more than gratitude.

He is mine.

Elena grinned, unable to form a clear greeting as he passed behind her and greeted her father.

Have I nothing to say—or too much?

She clenched her teeth.

Had she even thanked him for saving her life?

She leaned back and observed as the seating usher led him to his chair at the end of the dais. Sir Albert and the other men were seated at the front of her table, near Sir Jurian.

The tables were filled with guests when the king arrived.

The king's herald pounded his long stave on the dais. "All rise for King Edward and Queen Philippa."

Her father helped her to her feet as the king, and his family took their seats on the dais.

"Please enjoy the bounty of the season," King Edward said after the royal family was seated.

Trenchers filled with succulent goose, bread, and fall vegetables were carried to the tables by the kitchen staff. Soon, musicians, dancers, and tumblers performed in succession between the long tables.

Elena's attention could not be held by the performers, and she wanted no more to eat. Her attention turned to the dais. She watched with longing as her knight spoke to the young queen. Perchance, she would have a moment to speak with him once the tables were cleared.

When the dessert of baked apples and sweetbreads were served, carolers walked through the gathering chanting Christmas rhymes.

When the singers wandered from the banquet hall, the king's herald pounded his staff on the dais. "The king will now hear the Champion's request." The herald bowed to King Edward.

The lords and ladies grew quiet.

Elena scooted her chair backward so she could see around the people in front of her, but she shouldn't have worried. When Sir Jurian came to his feet, his gaze immediately met hers.

Her knight bowed to the king. "Your Majesty, the treasure of your bounty has overfilled my cup this day. Truly, your generosity is more than legend." Jurian glanced from the king to Elena, and then to Sir Albert, who sat first at the table before him. "If it pleases Your Highness, I shall pass the Champion's Boon to my patron, whose colors I carried today. Sir Albert Clavel."

The king nodded to Jurian, then looked to Sir Albert as he came to his feet and faced the dais.

"Your Majesty." Sir Albert bowed.

Around Elena, the guests erupted in whispers. More than a few glances and grins were tossed her way.

Heloise spoke with Warner, a troubled expression on her face, but her father shushed her, then reached over and placed his warm hand over Elena's.

Sir Albert cleared his throat. "Sir Jurian Locke took pity on an old man and agreed that should he win the Champion's Boon he would allow me to make a request that has been close to my heart for some time." The old knight knelt before the dais. "The land and manor granted to me by your father shall become a cold and lonely place once my former squire, now my friend and knight, Sir Reginald Vale leaves for Wales. I do not want to be alone in my dotage, without an heir to my name."

"Speak then, Sir Albert. What is it you wish? If it is within my power to grant you your heart's desire, by the skill and bravery of your champion, I shall."

Elena suddenly knew what Sir Albert would request from the king. He had asked it of her father several times and pleaded with her to accept his hand in marriage. In return, the Earl of Hawthorn's estate would grow larger with the land Sir Albert owned. She gripped her father's hand and leaned forward to whisper in his ear. "No, please, father. I cannot—"

"Hush." He gathered both her cold hands in his. "All will be well. Sir Albert is a fine man."

Elena's gaze sought Jurian's, and the sorrow in his eyes told her he also knew what Sir Albert would request. Tears stung as she stared at the back of Sir Albert's head.

"Your Majesty, if it pleases you, I would ask that you make an old knight's last years less lonely and grant me the boon of an heir." Sir Albert looked from King Edward to Jurian. "Please allow me to name Sir Jurian Locke as my heir to the Clavel manor and lands."

"Done!" King Edward proclaimed with a broad smile.

The room erupted in conversation and shouts of congratulations to Sir Jurian and Sir Albert. Elena lost sight of her knight when guests stood.

"My lady…" Kelsey's voice whispered close to her ear.

Elena met her friend's raw gaze. *She's been crying.* "Kelsey, what's wrong?"

"It's Piers. Come with me, please." Kelsey handed Elena her cane.

"Father, I'll be with Kelsey," Elena spoke, but her father only glanced back and nodded. He and Heloise had their heads close together.

Kelsey helped Elena stand, and they wove through the guests toward the door. Tables were being cleared and moved to the side as the musicians gathered in the corner. The two young women left the noisy hall and passed into the relative quiet of the entryway.

"This way, My Lady. We must hurry." Kelsey sniffed and held Elena's arm as they hurried down a short hall to the base of the stairs.

In the darkness, a body lay lifeless at the foot of the stairs.

Kelsey cried out and ran forward. She fell to her knees beside the motionless figure. "Piers?"

"He'll be fine. Like I told you both, Piers is a sore disappointment to me, preferring the company of maids to that of an heiress. However, I am not so old that I cannot make more sons."

Elena moved back as Milton Ramsey descended the stair. The light from the wall sconce reflected in his eyes as they focused on her. "My Lady, if you would come with me."

CHAPTER NINE

Jurian made his way across the crowded room. Dinner guests stood in groups of two and three talking. Some guests formed circles in the center of the room in preparation for the dance. Jurian's height gave him an advantage, but he couldn't find Elena seated along the wall. When he glimpsed her father near the musicians, he made his way to the Earl's side.

"My Lord." Jurian nodded a greeting. "I hoped to speak with your daughter."

"Sir Jurian." Warner smiled and tipped his head. "Elena left with her maid after the king bestowed his boon. You have my profound congratulations."

"Thank you, My Lord." Jurian pressed his lips and looked at the hall exit. "Do you know where Elena and her maid may have gone?"

"I thought they'd gone to the privy." Warner shrugged. "I'm surprised they haven't returned."

Something is amiss. The surprise of Sir Albert's request had stunned Jurian. He and Elena had exchanged glances at that moment and he thought—

nay, he *knew* she desired to speak with him.

"Pray, forgive me, sir." Jurian bowed back from her father. "I shall step out and check on their welfare."

"I'll accompany you." Warner's brows drew together. "They've been too long away from the feast, even for young ladies." He kissed Heloise's hand. "Wait for me here."

The two men left the din of the hall and paused in the entry. Palace staff rushed to clear the last remnants of dinner before the musicians struck their first notes.

Warner pointed toward the shadows near the stairs. "There." He skirted a line of white-coated kitchen staff and hurried down the short hall, Jurian close behind.

At the base of the stairs, a man leaned against the stone wall, blood running from his scalp down his face.

The young maid wept as she pressed a cloth to his head. "He swore he only wished to speak with her."

"Elena?" Warner demanded. "Who wished to speak with her?"

Jurian shifted uneasily. His gaze darted toward the second floor. "Where are they now?"

The maid shook her head. "Elena and I found Piers at the base of the staircase. As soon as we arrived, Pier's father, Lord Ramsay, took Elena by the waist and drew her up the steps." She covered her mouth as she wept. "I beg your forgiveness, My Lord. I never thought he would harm Elena or his own son."

Jurian rounded the group and climbed the steps three at a time. On the second floor, he paused to listen. Eyes closed. Senses alive and attuned to his love. No scent of her fragrance or sound of her breath touched him. *Higher then.* He raced up the second flight of stairs and stopped on the darkened third-floor.

A chill draft blew down the hall as he inspected one direction and then the other. The Earl's footsteps climbing the stair below didn't distract him. Down the hall to his right lay a familiar object. A cry of protest reached him as he spotted her skirt rounding the corner of the next passage.

Adrenaline sparked Jurian's heart. He raced down the hall and snatched Elena's crutch from the stone floor without breaking his stride.

Elena's muffled cry spurred him on. His heart pounded in his chest. He didn't pause to try the latch. Instead, he threw his weight against the wooden door and burst into the room.

Milton Ramsey held both of Elena's wrists above her head as he pressed himself against her. Her back crushed against the wall.

Red marks marred the white skin of her face and neck where Milton had grasped her roughly to hold her still. His eyes widened and he yanked Elena in front of him as a shield against Jurian's rage. "I've had her already. She's ruined for anyone but me."

Elena shook her head. "No, he lies."

Jurian advanced toward them and his gaze dropped to Elena's tear-filled eyes. "I believe you." His eyes narrowed as he turned his attention to Milton Ramsey. "But it wouldn't matter to me if you had."

"I shall tell everyone. The king will demand she and I wed."

"You shall tell no tales." Jurian took another step into the room. "This is the last moment of your life, Milton Ramsey. Make your peace with God." His eyes shifted to Elena. *Now, my love.*

As though she read his mind, Elena allowed her leg give way, becoming dead weight in Ramsey's arms. Her head dropped forward, away from his shoulder as she sagged toward the ground.

Jurian flipped the crutch in his hand so the thick arm support faced Ramsey. He swung the heavy carved wood like a weighted mace upward, catching Milton beneath the chin with deadly accuracy.

Milton Ramsey's neck snapped with the force of the blow. He collapsed backward as Elena, released from his grip, fell forward.

Jurian dropped the crutch and fell to his knees, gathering Elena in his arms. "Are you well? Did he harm you?"

Elena shook her head and clung to Jurian's shoulders. "He only threatened me." Her dark gaze rose to meet his. "But if you hadn't come—"

"Be at ease, my love." Jurian touched his knuckles to her soft cheek. "No one shall threaten you again."

"Ramsey's actions make no sense to me." Elena held Jurian's hand against her face and stared into his eyes. "Why would Piers' father wish to ruin me?"

"He planned to force your hand in marriage." Her father spoke from inside the doorway. "To ensure his child inherited the Hawthorn lands and title."

Jurian helped Elena to her feet and handed her the crutch.

Her hands shook as she took it and tucked it beneath her arm.

"I would never have guessed he would go to such lengths." Warner rubbed his face and stared at Milton's sightless eyes. "The king will need to be told what occurred here."

"The king will be apprised." Roger Mortimer, the Earl of March, stood outside the door. "No doubt the Ramsey land will pay forfeit for this foul deed." Mortimer smoothed his jacket, his face grim with loathing.

"My Lord." The Earl of Hawthorn bowed his head to the king's adviser. "How did you know where to find us?"

Mortimer scowled. "In the entry, at the foot of the stairs, I found Ramsey's lad and a distraught maid. They directed me up the stairs." He indicated Milton Ramsey's corpse. "I'm not surprised to find Ramsey's vile plan thwarted by our champion."

Jurian exchanged glances with Elena's father. "What would you have us do, My Lord?"

"Do? Why, return to the feast." Roger Mortimer moved back and held out his arm to the stairs. "No need to bother young Edward about this foulness tonight. This incident shall be handled with discretion, of course." He waved his hand and two guards came out of the shadow. "Be merry. Enjoy the celebration."

Elena trembled as she moved across the hall.

Jurian shook his head. "This won't do." He swept her up in his arms as her father took her cane. "I don't want you to fall, my dear."

"I can manage, honestly. What will people say?" Elena protested.

Her father passed the couple and paused at the stairs. "Let them say what they like. He's your knight. You can do with him as you please." Warner continued down the stairs, his voice floated back to the couple. "If he wants to carry you around like a prize purse, I say let him. There's not a man downstairs who could make him put you down, I'd wager."

"At least let me carry you to the bottom of the stair. You're shaken. It would be far too easy for you to fall." Jurian looked into Elena's dark eyes and saw Agaria's soul move in their depths. "Besides, your father is right. Not a man in this castle could take you from me. Only you have that power. Shall I set you down?"

"Nay," her voice a whisper as her eyes searched his. "You may carry me to the base of the stairs, my knight."

"As my lady wishes." Jurian chuckled and descended the stairs.

Piers and Kelsey were gone from the entry hall. Instead, Elena's crutch set propped against the wall.

Jurian lowered her to her feet and she placed the wooden staff beneath her arm.

"Shall we, my lady?" He took a step, then paused and looked up. "Isn't that mistletoe hanging from the beam?"

"It is." Elena nodded. "A nasty plant. It grows on the Hawthorn trees all about our Essex estate."

"Mistletoe likes apple and oaks trees best." Jurian smiled at Elena. "Your Hawthorn trees are blessed to have such a fortunate plant upon them."

"What do you mean?"

Jurian reached up and touched the berries. "It is said mistletoe's white berries are the pearl-like tears that Frigga, the Goddess of Love, cried for her son, Balder, when he had been restored to life. In her joy, she kissed everyone who passed beneath the tree on which it grew." Jurian plucked a snowy berry and placed the white pearl in Elena's hand. "Frigga decreed that whoever should stand beneath her mistletoe would come to no harm, and take only a single kiss—as a token of love."

Jurian lowered his head and touched Elena's lips with a gentle kiss. Her soft lips parted easily at the pressure of his mouth. *My love.* Emotion crushed his chest. He lifted his head to catch his breath, only to find her arm wrapped around his neck, holding him close.

"A single kiss?" she whispered, her lips brushed against his when she spoke.

"I took but one kiss," he breathed into her mouth.

"Then I shall take one as well." Her crutch clattered to the floor as she wrapped her other arm around his neck.

He lifted her from her feet as their kiss deepened. The taste of her lips ignited memories of her past lives, and gave him a promise of their life to come. Both his curse and his joy were forever bound to Agaria's soul. Now, in Elena's arms, his life could begin again. Passion ignited inside his chest. His love, as evergreen as mistletoe leaves, and as pure as the white mistletoe berry.

* * *

Near the hall, Heloise nudged Warner. "Come inside. Give your daughter a moment's privacy with her knight."

Warner chuckled and lifted his wife's hand to his lips. "I thought the mistletoe would work well there. Jurian's a smart lad."

"And you left her crutch beneath it. You're terribly clever as well."

Warner smiled, tucked his wife's hand inside his arm and led her toward the ball room. "Sir Albert will be pleased, I dare say. Perhaps by this time next year we shall have a marriage."

Heloise looked back at the couple. "I don't think you should wait that long, Warner."

Warner turned just as Jurian set Elena on her feet and reached for her crutch. Their faces flushed with delight as they paused for another brief kiss before he handed her the cane.

"Mmm. Perhaps you're right." Warner grinned at the joy on his daughter's face. "I never thought to see her this happy."

"Warner, look." Heloise pointed to the mistletoe above their heads.

"Clever girl." The Earl of Hawthorn murmured as he kissed his wife. "My very clever girl."

Also by C. Marie Bowen

~ *Novels* ~

Aubrielle's Call
(**Timeless Quest** / France – 1939)
***

Soul of the Witch Series – 1875
Passage, Book 1
Prophecy, Book 2
Paradox, Book 3

~ *Novellas* ~

The Hunter Chronicles
Hunter's Gamble – 1865
Hunter and Lily Graham - 1872
The Kid in Black – 1872
***

Hawthorn and Mistletoe
(**Timeless Quest** / England – 1328)

~

The Corsair's Tempest
(**Timeless Quest** / Caribbean – 1701)

~ *Coming soon* ~

Pyromancer, Book 4 – 1872
Soul of the Witch Series

Her mortal crisis. His immortal curse.
And the call he's compelled to answer.

Aubrielle's Call

C. MARIE BOWEN

Aubrielle's Call

By C. Marie Bowen

The world careens towards war...

Consumed with grief by the death of his soul mate, immortal John Larson trades his spurs for the scent of the sea and the life of a merchant marine.

Condemned by an ancient curse, he's bound to await her rebirth, for a threat to her life, and for the magical summons that will draw him to her side.

In the heart of Paris, Aubrielle Cohen struggles to survive. Resolved to support her dying father, she sells flowers from a horse-drawn cart to tourists, who now flee the onset of war.

Beneath the Eiffel Tower, she learns a hard lesson about trust and meets a stranger whose presence evokes an irrational yearning in her soul.

As the Nazi war machine stands poised to invade Aubrielle's homeland, John must gain her trust, defend her life, and rekindle the passion he hopes still stirs deep within her heart

Aubrielle's Call

Chapter One

September 1939

Able Seaman John Larson swung onto his lower rack as the overhead light in the seamen's quarters winked off, and the red light came on. *The Yankee Dream* would make Boston Harbor the day after tomorrow. The run from Panama should prove profitable for the small merchant vessel. Lucrative enough, the shipmaster had hinted, that there might be a bonus to the crew's regular wages.

John closed his eyes and prayed for a dreamless rest. A nightly ritual ever since the death of his wife, almost twenty years ago. How long would her face haunt him?

Until the magic beckons and I find her again.

As memories edged into dreams, he watched his wife call flame to her hand. In the glow of the fire, her perfect silhouette stole his breath. Her smile and sparkling eyes nearly broke his heart.

Alyse, my love. How I miss you.

Emotion closed his throat, and he clenched his teeth, awake once more.

John hunched his shoulders and rolled to his side. A seaman's rack didn't fit a man his size. To curl his six-foot-five frame onto a six-foot long bunk became another nightly torture. Still, work on a ship offered enough change from working cattle. These reflections only plagued him at night.

After he lost had Alyse, he buried the man he'd been beside her. He chose a new name. A new profession. A new life. The in-between years stretched before him. The years, decades, centuries, after his soul mate's death.

What if I never feel her call again?

The recollections of their recent life together were still too raw and painful to bear. Eventually, he would cherish the memory of Alyse as he did all the lives she had lived, back to the beginning.

Back to Agaria.

Agaria sim Biraci.

My life changed forever because I loved Agaria and rejected another.

As if summoned, the sharp specter of the Druidess Nescato scraped across his mind. Her jealous, contorted face encircled by the Biraci tribe's most sacred pelts. The embodiment of evil. Bitter with envy, she raised her staff to the heavens, spoke her curse, and then pointed the staff at him and Agaria.

Nescato cursed his soul to endure the centuries alone, unable to love another. Bound forever to await his soul mate's rebirth, for a threat to her life, and for the magical summons that would draw him to her side. Not always able to reach her or save her, he would forever be compelled to try.

He pushed the image of the sorceress away and rolled to his other side, seeking a comfortable spot, both on the bed and in his heart.

"Hey, Big John, you're rocking the rack," Elmer Jones called down from above.

"He's rocking the ship," Fred Harmon said from across the way.

"Sorry," John muttered.

Lie still. Rest.

The motion of the ship relaxed him, lulled him to sleep. At first, a deep, restful emptiness soothed and replenished his mind and body.

And then he dreamed.

He stood the first watch, waiting in a darkened room. Silent as the night, Alyse joined him, slipping her small hand into his.

Further back.

Alyse laughed when she took his arm, and he escorted her to the family dinner table.

A sweet reminiscence.

Their first kiss. A promise made a hundred times over. *I love only you.*

His dream darkened.

He waited inside a circle scored in the dirt. The intense heat of a summer sun beat down on his shoulders. Others fought beside him, but dust obscured his vision. He wiped a sleeve across his eyes, and Alyse stood before him. Fire cradled in her hands. Hatred bled from her eyes like tears.

Out of the shadows crawled a monster. The threat to his beloved's life. The reason for his summons. This prophetic evil had threatened Alyse since the day she'd been born.

John raised his rifle and took aim. The name he once called himself rang through the apparitions of sleep. *"Jim, wait!"*

"Wake up, son." Fred nudged John with his boot. "It's time for morning muster."

John rolled from his rack and stretched, pressing his palms against the overhead steam pipes. Most of his shipmates had already dressed and headed aft for breakfast. He pulled on his dungarees, buttoned his shirt, and followed Fred up the ladder to the main deck.

At muster, Bosun Garza assigned John to mend the mooring lines damaged while in Panama. When he finished that task, he was to chip and paint the bollards with young Elmer.

Clear blue sky and southerly winds stayed with them as they sailed up the coastal waters. The crew moved about their tasks with a light heart. Tomorrow they'd make port.

At evening mess, John consumed a bowl of soup and a slice of bread.

"Will you join us in town tonight, John?" Elmer asked.

"Of course, he will." Fred dabbed at the last bit of soup in his dish with a crust of bread. "We'll unload the ship, collect our pay, and depart. Ain't that right, Big John?"

John shook his head at his friends. "How can I argue with the two of you?"

Elmer, a farm boy from Nebraska with a large head and a shock of white hair, rubbed his hands together in anticipation.

The oldest of the three, Fred took a sip of his coffee and laughed at Elmer.

After another night at sea, the morning found them moored in Boston Harbor. The long task of unloading the cargo and waiting in line to see the ship's purser seized most of the day. They crossed the gangway at dusk and headed for Gull's Tavern.

Early evening customers filled the bar. The friends found a small table near the back.

"I'll buy the first round," Fred said and made his way through the jam-packed bar.

Elmer pointed. "There's a barmaid."

The buxom server shoved mugs of brew across a table filled with sailors. She pulled a pencil from her rolled curls, prepared to take their orders.

"She's busy." John pulled out a chair. "Let's wait for Fred."

On the shelf behind them, a radio played a swing melody. As the song ended, a Glen Miller tune began to play.

"Look, they're dancing." Elmer nudged him and pointed at three couples near the bar.

Fred wove through the crowd with mugs of beer and set them on the small table. "Drink up, shipmates. Next round's on John."

"Are we going back to Panama, have you heard?" Elmer asked Fred.

Fred took a swig from his mug and wiped the foam from his mustache. "Seems likely. Bananas, coffee, and sugar sell well in the States. Master Riley welcomes the profit, and so my friends, do I." He smacked his lips and took another drink.

The music changed to a slower song and a woman's lilting voice crooned about the memory of a lost love. John's stomach clenched each time they played this song. It reminded him of Agaria. He drank his beer in silence and watched the dancers.

"Will you stay on *The Dream*, Big John?" Elmer asked.

He shrugged. "No reason not to. The master is fair and the pay, as you say, is good."

The barmaid offered to bring another round.

John pulled a bill from his pocket. "I'll buy."

As the dark-haired server returned with their mugs, the radio changed from music to news. Several patrons shouted for her to switch the station to dance music, but she hesitated, listening to the announcer.

"News today from Great Britain. German forces have invaded Poland. German planes have bombed Polish cities, including the capital, Warsaw. The attack came without any warning or declaration of war. Britain and France have declared war on Germany in support of Poland. They have mobilized their forces in preparation to wage war on Germany for the second time this century."

A cold chill ran down John's arms.

The barmaid reached for the dial. "I hate those lousy Krauts," she told John with a smile and a wink as the first notes of a jazz tune played on the radio. She let the music play and took an order from the next table.

The noise in the bar became muted and distant. A familiar high-pitched whine bled into John's brain.

His mouth went dry as his heart thundered alongside the shriek in his ear. A cold sweat plagued his brow.

It's been only twenty years since I buried Alyse.

He shook his head and stared at Elmer and Fred.

The in-between always lasts longer.

The men talked and laughed. Elmer nudged Fred and pointed across the bar, but when they spoke, John heard nothing.

The call has come so soon. She must be a child.

His stomach twisted with certainty as pain pierced between his eyes and shot through to the back of his skull. John set his mug on the table and missed. Released from his hand, the beaker fell and then slowed to a stop in mid-air. The beer's foamy head froze in its splash toward the floor. His hand, a hairsbreadth from the handle.

In the next instant, time resumed.

The mug shattered and the barmaid spun in surprise.

The pressure in his head expanded, pushing outward until his vision filled with white light. The pain contracted to a single point above his right eye.

"I'll get that." The barmaid pulled a towel from her skirt pocket and tossed it over the spill.

"You feel all right, John?" Fred raised an eyebrow and took another swig.

John squeezed his eyes shut and pressed the heel of his palms against his eyelids "I'll be all right." He lowered his hands. When he moved, the point of pain sliced across his forehead. He tilted his head the other way until the sting settled between his brows. He didn't have to step outside to know he faced east-northeast.

Across the sea, Agaria calls.

Chapter Two

Is she in Poland?

John nodded to the barmaid as she replaced his beer.

She used her shoe to sweep the towel and glass across the floor, away from the dancers.

The stinging point on his forehead would be a distraction until he set eyes on Agaria.

Or whoever she is in her new life.

The adrenaline spike in his chest would ease once his journey toward her began.

He brushed a hand along the back of his neck. There would be no way to reach her for days, even weeks, and he had no idea where to find her.

His heart clenched.

Damn.

John gripped the handle of his mug and raised the foamy brew to his lips.

The white-haired young sailor emptied his glass and chuckled at the dancers. He elbowed Fred and pointed. "See the blonde? I knew a girl in Toledo who moved like that."

John drank his beer and watched the blonde dancer. He remembered a conversation he'd had with a curly-haired blonde, a lifetime ago. She had knowledge of the future and warned of wars that would encompass the entire world. Wars fought with weapons that didn't exist in the late nineteenth century. She'd been right.

He and Alyse had learned of events in the Great War by reading newspaper reports from the safety of their Denver home. Thankful for once, they could never conceive a child.

The second war, his friend had warned, would sweep across Europe in what the Germans would call a blitzkrieg. The death toll would be astronomical, especially in Poland.

John drank his beer. If his love dwelt in Poland, she could already be beyond his reach. Even so, she lived. As long as her heart continued to beat, he'd feel her call, and the direction he must follow.

He scrubbed his hand over his face. *I'll have to cross the Atlantic.*

Once in Europe, he'd have a better idea where to find her.

Fred cleared his throat and raised an eyebrow. "You're less than fine I'd say. What's on your mind, son?"

John pressed his lips and took a deep breath. "I won't be sailing on *The Dream* to Panama." He leaned back and ran his hand through his hair. "I need to find a ship making a North Atlantic run."

"What?" Elmer set his mug down hard. "Are you mad?"

"Why rush off to war?" Fred narrowed his eyes and put his beaker on the table.

John shook his head. "Not war. Not for me." He waved his thumb at the radio. "But war means more ships sailing to Europe, more profit."

"Could be." Elmer shrugged. His attention returned to the dancers.

"I'd guess you have family in Europe?" Fred held his gaze and sipped his brew.

John rolled his shoulders and gave his friend a slow nod. "I do." He looked away and rubbed at a point on his forehead. "And I can't just listen to radio reports and speculation. I need to find her." He glanced at Fred. "Find them."

Fred tipped his head toward one of the tables filled with men. "Ask those shipmates where they're bound." He gave a nod to several men at the bar. "Those men, as well. The Gull is as good a place as any to find a ship across the pond."

John gave Fred a pat on his shoulder and rose from his chair. There were five men at the table dressed in sailor's dungarees. He stopped beside them and nodded. "Good evening, mates. I'm looking for work on a North Atlantic run to Britain or any port along the European coast."

Five ruddy faces lifted to John.

"Nothing goes to Britain now, because of their tariffs." A husky man at the table jutted his chin at John. "You a stoker?

John shook his head. "Deckhand."

"Talk to the men at the bar." One of the sailors pointed with his thumb over his shoulder.

"Thanks." John scanned the bar.

Two mariners threw down bills for their tab and rose to leave.

"Gentlemen," John said. "I heard you might have a berth for a deckhand heading to Britain."

One sailor shook his head and shrugged into his

jacket. "Sorry, mate."

The other man narrowed his eyes at John. "You might ask in some of the taverns on the south end of the pier." He winked and left the bar.

John returned to their table.

"No luck?" Fred asked.

"No." John picked up his mug. "But they suggested I try south along the pier."

Young Elmer drained his glass, stood and rubbed his hands together. "I'm going to dance with the blonde. Wish me luck." He two-stepped his lanky frame away from their table. His focus on the dancers.

Fred shook his head at the younger man. "That boy needs watching. Have a seat, son. You can ask around tomorrow. The south end's no place for a lad alone at night."

"This can't wait." The adrenaline punch to his gut kept John on his feet. He couldn't sit still. "I'm going to walk down the pier and ask around." John threw down money for their next round and ducked outside into the night.

The sharp point of pain on his head swung around his skull like a compass arrow spinning north. He crossed the street and headed south along the pier. To his right, warehouses and darkened alleyways lined the waterfront, a counterpoint to the brightly lit harbor. Past the warehouses, music, and bawdy laughter echoed down a side street. He put his back to the pier and walked up the dead end road. All around, the scent of the harbor hung heavy in the night air.

Three taverns competed in the cul-de-sac.

Several men passed by, headed to the dock, and gaped at John. They commented on his height and burst into laughter.

John ignored their amusement.

As he entered the first bar, the shatter of glass in the cul-de-sac made him pause.

From the tavern across the way, a mariner fell backward into the street.

Four men pursued him out the door and stood on the sidewalk, mocking the fallen man.

Without hesitation, John turned from the doorway and into the street. His long stride took him to the man who lay on his back rubbing his jaw.

"Are you injured?" John asked.

The man's eyebrows rose as he looked up at John's face.

"I'll do, friend." He raised his hand and John hoisted him to his feet.

The men, clustered on the sidewalk, followed their leader into the street. "Found a friend, Sweeney?"

"He's no part in this, Taylor. Hell, I've no part in this." Sweeney brushed his hands along his thighs and reached down to grab his cap. "She asked me to dance. I didn't know the whore belonged to you."

Taylor charged Sweeney and came to an abrupt halt against John's hand.

"Easy, shipmate," John said to the thick-necked man.

Taylor's face flushed. "She's not a whore," he yelled at Sweeney. Spittle flew from his mouth, and he wiped the back of his fist across his lips.

"I bet she's wondering where you've gone,"

John said in a calm voice. "You should take your friends back inside and buy your lady friend a drink."

Taylor's bloodshot eyes focused on John. "This doesn't concern you, mate."

"Not yet. I only offer you a bit of good advice." John eyed Taylor's friends as they moved to flank him and Sweeney. "You don't want this fight."

"Screw you, Goliath." Taylor barked and swung wildly at John. He missed by four inches. He swung again, but John's arm held him further than the burly man's reach.

"Tell your friends to step back," John demanded.

Sweeney shuffled up beside John; fists raised. "Leave off, Taylor. You'll get us thrown in the brig over a whore."

"Get 'em," Taylor yelled, and two of his friends stepped to either side of John.

John lifted Taylor and tossed him into his nearest man. Both went down with a grunt and rolled in the dirt.

At John's side, Sweeney dealt Taylor's other comrade a hard right to the nose and a left uppercut to his gut. The man sat down and gasped for breath.

The last of Taylor's friends took a step back, spun on their heels, and raced into the bar.

Taylor struggled to his feet and glared at John. "I'll remember you." He shook his finger at John as he hastened into the bar, his friends close behind.

"We'd best move on." Sweeney brushed his clothing and walked toward the pier. "Shore Patrol will be around." He stopped at the end of the street. "Come along," he called to John. "There's a quiet bar round the corner. I owe you a drink."

John cast a last glance at the doorway where Taylor and his friends had entered. "John Larson, able seaman on *The Yankee Dream*." He held out his hand and fell into step beside Sweeney.

"Bosun Sweeney on the *Giselle-Marie* but my friends call me Pete." They walked south along the pier. "*Yankee Dream*? Is she docked on the south end?"

"No." John shook his head. "We docked north. Just in from a Panama run. I expect Master Riley will make a return run as soon as *The Dream* is loaded."

"What're you doing on the south pier?" Sweeney pointed down the next street, and they changed direction.

"Looking for work on a ship bound for Britain."

Sweeney opened the door of a quiet tavern and ushered John inside. They ordered a draft from the bartender and found a seat at an open booth.

When their drinks arrived, Sweeney took a long draw on his mug and gave John an appraising look. "No ships are bound for Britain, mate. Their tariffs make it unprofitable, and now, their declaration of war makes it illegal."

"Illegal?" John ran his hand through his thick dark hair. "I thought the Brits would want to buy arms."

"I'm sure they do." Sweeney set his mug on the table and cocked one eyebrow at John. "But the U.S. doesn't trade with belligerent nations, at least not according to Roosevelt and Congress." He wiped at a wet spot on the dark wood tabletop. "A little thing called the Neutrality Act makes transporting goods, passengers, and arms to a country at war a federal crime."

"You're saying there's no way to sail to Europe?" John rubbed at the stinging spot on his forehead. "I can't accept that."

"No, mate. I'm not saying you can't sail to Britain. I'm saying it's illegal." Sweeney rested his arm along the back of the bench and eyed John. "Able seaman, you said, and good in a fight, by my own eyes. Tell me—" Sweeney leaned forward, elbows on the table. "If I knew a master, who wanted to help the Brits and Frogs, and make a bit of cash for his crew on the side, would you be interested?"

"Aye," John replied without hesitation. "I would."

Sweeney grinned. "That's good, mate." He paused as two sailors entered the bar and moved to a table in the back. "It's too crowded this early," Sweeney said in a low voice into his half-empty glass. "Come back at midnight. Tell the bartender you're to meet with me. He'll give you directions." He finished his beer and set the mug down hard on the table. "Don't be late." He turned his collar up and slipped out the door.

About the Author

Award winning author, C. (Connie) Marie
Bowen writes the kind of stories she loves to read,
paranormal fantasy and time travel with heroes
from the past, present, and future. Her stories are
crafted to contain an element of magic, suspense
and romance. Each tale is an extension or prequel to
another. She has created a series of novels and
novellas with characters her readers have grown to
love.

Connie grew up in Denver, telling stories to her
friends who say they're not a bit surprised she
became a writer. However, that didn't happen right
away. Her stories of magic and adventure were put
on the back-burner but remained close to her heart.

She moved from Denver to Wichita, Kansas, and
then finally settled in North Texas to raise her sons.
Connie earned a certification in Architectural
Drafting and Design and worked her way up
through retail design to Project Manager at an
Architect and Engineering firm in Fort Worth,
Texas. As a person who paid attention to detail and
cared about her surroundings, she earned a Green
Building Certification as a LEED (Leadership in
Energy and Environmental Design) Accredited
Professional.

Her first novel, Passage, won First Place in the
Paranormal Romance category in Indiana's Golden

Opportunity contest in 2014. In 2015, her novels Passage and Prophecy were both nominated for RONE awards in the Time Travel and Paranormal categories, respectively.

Connie resides in Texas with her wonderfully understanding husband and two rescue pets, a friendly feline named Abby and comedy prone Chiweenie named Russo.

She is a member of Texas Authors, Inc.

Keep up with new releases on her website: www.cmariebowen.com or follow her on Amazon.

A Note from the Author

I sincerely appreciate you reading my book. If you enjoyed this book, please recommend it to a friend or leave a rating/review on your favorite book site. Words cannot express how much this helps authors like myself.

Please feel free to reach out and connect with me on the sites below. I would love to hear from you!

Website: CMarieBowen.com

Facebook: author.CMBowen

Twitter: @CMarieTexas

Pinterest: CMarieBowen

Instagram: c.marie.bowen

www.ingramcontent.com/pod-product-compliance
Lightning Source LLC
Chambersburg PA
CBHW070457130626
46555CB00003B/1049